Red Water

# 少年駭客
## 之綠色事件簿

作者 Antoinette Moses
譯者 李璞良

## ABOUT THIS BOOK

For the Student   🎧 Listen to the story and do some
activities on your Audio CD.
💬 Talk about the story.

For the Teacher

Go to our Readers Resource site for information on using
readers and downloadable Resource Sheets, photocopiable
Worksheets, and Tapescripts. www.helblingreaders.com

For lots of great ideas on using Graded Readers consult
Reading Matters, the Teacher's Guide to using Helbling
Readers.

### Structures

| | |
|---|---|
| Modal verb would | Non-defining relative clauses |
| I'd love to … | Present perfect continuous |
| Future continuous | Used to / would |
| Present perfect future | Used to / used to doing |
| Reported speech / verbs / questions | Second conditional |
| Past perfect | Expressing wishes and regrets |
| Defining relative clauses | |

Structures from lower levels are also included.

# CONTENTS

**When did you first know you wanted to write?**

I can't remember a time when I didn't want to write. I first wrote a play, which I performed with my family at Christmas, when I was eight years old. Even when I did other things I always knew I was a writer and I was just filling in time until I could sit down and write.

**You mention plays. Do you still write plays or just stories?**

I write lots of stories for English language learners and I also write plays as I like the challenge of describing people through what they say and do. It's very different from writing fiction, but very exciting when you see actors playing characters you have invented.

How do you begin a story?

Well I don't wait for inspiration. Often I begin with an issue, for example something that makes me angry or worried. Then I think about the characters. Who would be involved in this issue? What kind of people are affected or get involved in it?

Why did you write this story?

There is a lot of discussion in the papers at the moment about the environment and carbon trade, and it is a subject that has interested me for many years.

Have you ever been to Africa?

I've been to North Africa several times, and I once sailed in a boat all the way round Africa to Kenya and fell in love with the continent. I feel that what happens in Africa is important for all of us.

**1** The story, *Red Water*, takes place in England and the Ivory Coast. Listen to the information about the Ivory Coast and answer the questions.

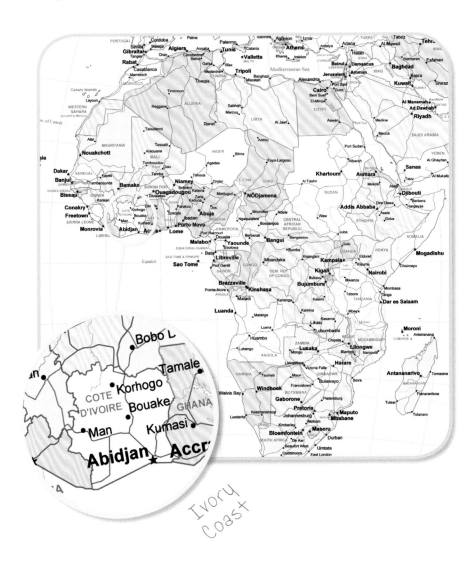

Ivory Coast

1   The Ivory Coast is in ……… Africa.
    a East                    b West                    c North

2   Which of the following countries doesn't border with the Ivory Coast?
    a The Gambia         b Guinea         c Ghana

3   The climate is hot and wet from ………
    a November to March   b March to May       c June to October

4   Mont Nimba is a ……… in the Ivory Coast.
    a lake                    b mountain                c forest

5   The population of the Ivory Coast is ………
    a 17.6 million         b 70.6 million         c 16.7 million

6   People in the Ivory Coast live until around the age of ………
    a 59                      b 69                      c 49

7   Yamoussoukro is the ……… of the Ivory Coast.
    a largest city         b capital city         c former capital city

8   Which of the following can the Ivory Coast not export?
    a diamonds            b cocoa               c rubber

2 With a partner write a quiz about your country. Then give the quiz
  to another pair to do.

**3** Read these quotes from the story and answer the questions.

> a  . . . he just smashed his way into the apartment. He didn't say his name, but his purpose was clear. What he wanted was silence. And that was what he got. He bought silence with fear.
>
> b  "That is extremely serious," agreed the inspector. "We've got every available police officer looking for your sister. But I'm afraid it's a question of whether we can find her in time."

1  What kind of story is it? Tick.
☐ Thriller   ☐ Adventure   ☐ Horror   ☐ Romance

2  What do you think takes place in the story? Tick two items.
☐ A murder   ☐ A hijack   ☐ A kidnap   ☐ A robbery

**4** Look at the pictures below. Describe the people.

1  What do they look like?
2  What kind of personalities do you think they have got?
3  What do you think their professions are?

Daniel

Mr Johnson

Tricia

**5** Who do you think is the villain of the story? Give reasons.

**6** Check if you know the meaning of these words from the story.

- a memory stick
- b leaflets
- c emissions
- d global corporations
- e the races
- f dam
- g explosion
- h mine

**7** The words are all important to the story. Can you guess how? Use each of the words above to complete the sentences.

a They decided to produce ............. and hand them out outside the supermarket.

b Suddenly there was a huge ............. . Smoke and flames poured out of the building.

c They say that they are building a hydro-electric ............. there, to make electricity.

d These days the big ............. are more powerful than governments.

e Governments around the world have been asked to lower their ............. of greenhouse gases.

f Since he was ten he had worked down a ............. digging diamonds out of the ground.

g She copied all the information she needed from the computer onto her ............. .

h Her father owned a racehorse and he often brought his clients to ............. .

**8** Choose one of the sentences above. Continue the story from there.

1 prompt [prɑmpt] (v.) 促使；激勵
2 equatorial [ˌɛkwəˋtorɪəl] (a.) 赤道的
3 witness [ˋwɪtnɪs] (v.) 目擊
4 perpetrator [ˋpɝpəˏtretɚ] (n.) 行兇者
5 canopy [ˋkænəpɪ] (n.) 遮蓋物
6 blur [blɝ] (n.) 模糊；污點
7 muffled [ˋmʌfl̩d] (a.) 隱約的
8 thud [θʌd] (n.) 重擊聲
9 clump [klʌmp] (n.) 樹叢

On Thursday 12th May two apparently unrelated things happened within the same two minutes in two very different parts of the world.

"What's extraordinary . . ." says Tricia, looking back at that moment. She stops.

"Yes?" prompts[1] her mother.

"What's so incredible," Tricia continues, "is that they happened on the same day, at the same time. Don't you think?"

"I *don't* think," says her mother. "I try not to think. I just try to move on."

"I keep thinking, what if?" says Tricia. "What if one of those things hadn't happened? What if I . . .? I know, Mum," she says. "You can't go through life saying, 'what if?' – but just imagine . . . *what if?*"

\*    \*    \*    \*    \*    \*

The first event took place on a dusty red earth road that led to a small village in the heart of equatorial[2] Africa. It was an event witnessed[3] only by its perpetrators[4] and two gray parrots that rose screaming from the forest canopy[5] in a blur[6] of red tail-feathers. There was the sound of a gun firing. Three times. And then the muffled[7] thud[8] of a man's body being thrown into a clump[9] of thorn bushes.

To the men with the guns he wasn't a man; he was a job, a task. They never thought of him as a man. Nor did the men who had sent them. That was their mistake.

Every human has a name; every human has a story. This man, the man who had died, was called Winston. Winston worked for a large multinational company that had just sacked[1] him; and Winston was scared. That was why he'd left the city and was trying to escape to his village at the other end of the dusty red road.

He'd been born in that village, but had moved to the capital city to study, and then, later, after he had acquired[2] certificates[3] and a degree, he had stayed on to work there. In the city he had a wife and two children, and they were worried about him. His wife knew that something bad was going on, but for the sake[4] of the children she said nothing.

Winston's wife was a kind woman who loved her husband and her children. When the man came to her home, she knew something bad was going to happen. This man didn't say very much. He was a man of few words. He was called the Sweeper[5], and he was one of the two men who, on that Thursday morning, were carrying guns and climbing back into the Land Rover[6] on a dusty red earth road in Africa.

The Sweeper didn't knock on the door of Winston's home – he just smashed[7] his way into the apartment. He didn't say his name, but his purpose was clear. What he wanted was silence. And that was what he got. He bought silence with fear.

The Sweeper was a man who traded[8] in fear. He was a man who swept up problems. Winston was a problem, and the Sweeper got rid of[9] him. And now he was in Winston's home, and his message to Winston's wife was clear; he knew where she and the children lived.

Winston's wife understood. She bought her children's lives with silence, but she knew she couldn't buy her husband's life. It was already too late. That was why Winston's wife had wept[10] even before the news of Winston's death reached her. Winston was dead before he left the city, before he walked down the dusty red earth road.

Winston's wife loved her husband, but she did not speak out. Not then, or ever. She had to think about her children. The Sweeper relied[11] on this. He, and the men who paid him, the company men.

---

● ● ●

## Silence

- Winston's wife decides not to speak out against the Sweeper. Can you think of a time when you chose not to speak? Or when it would be best to say nothing?

---

1 sack [sæk] (v.) 開除
2 acquire [əˈkwaɪr] (v.) 獲得
3 certificate [səˈtɪfəkɪt] (n.) 結業證書
4 sake [sek] (n.) 理由
5 sweeper [ˈswipɚ] (n.) 清潔工
6 Land Rover 多用途越野車

7 smash [smæʃ] (v.) 猛衝；猛撞
8 trade [tred] (v.) 進行交易 (n.) 交易
9 get rid of 擺脫
10 weep [wip] (v.) 哭泣 ( 動詞三態：weep; wept; wept )
11 rely [rɪˈlaɪ] (v.) 依賴

The company knew that people would notice Winston's disappearance; they knew people would ask questions. Winston was popular; he had many friends. But the Sweeper made a mistake. He thought that no one would find Winston's body. He thought the ants would arrive first, and the rains. He thought Winston's wife would be silent and no one would know. He thought the job was done. But the Sweeper didn't know Winston's wife.

Winston's wife was intelligent[1] and she loved her children, but she cared about her husband, too. So, while she did not talk about the Sweeper, she did act. The day after the men visited her apartment, she went to the market as she always did, but this time she spoke quietly to a man selling fish. He was a man who was married to a woman whose sister was married to a man from Winston's village. That was how the information was passed back. Quietly. Invisibly[2]. Within a day the people of that village left their homes and walked along the dusty red road, where they found Winston's body.

The company told a different story. They said that Winston was depressed[3]. Then they issued[4] a statement[5] saying he was sacked because there were figures[6] that did not add up[7]. They implied[8] that Winston was a thief, though no one actually accused[9] him of this. The company said that Winston had disappeared.

---

1 intelligent [ɪnˋtɛlədʒənt] (a.) 聰明的
2 invisibly [ɪnˋvɪzəblɪ] (adv.) 看不見地
3 depressed [dɪˋprɛst] (a.) 感到沮喪的
4 issue [ˋɪʃju] (v.) 發布
5 statement [ˋstetmənt] (n.) 聲明
6 figure [ˋfɪgjɚ] (n.) 數字
7 add up 前後一致
8 imply [ɪmˋplaɪ] (v.) 暗指
9 accuse [əˋkjuz] (v.) 指控

The company thought it was rather inconvenient[1] that his body was found so soon. Bad luck. The villagers said the goats were feeding[2] near the thorn bushes. A goat boy found the body. It was the goats. It was bad luck.

The company did not think that Winston's wife could have asked someone to send goats along the path. She and her children were safe. The company thought it was bad luck. The Sweeper thought it was bad luck. He thought Winston's wife was too afraid to speak. He didn't think she had the courage to do anything. It was the goats. It was bad luck.

So the company changed its story. The new story was that Winston had killed himself. That was the story. But it was a strange story. A man walked along the road and then shot himself and jumped into a thorn bush. And there was no gun. The villagers mentioned[3] these details very quietly, because they had children. They understood men with guns; they knew about the Sweeper and men like him. Even quiet stories are heard. There are people who ask questions and listen and talk.

\*　　\*　　\*　　\*　　\*　　\*

---

1 inconvenient [ˌɪnkənˈvɪnjənt] (a.) 交通不便的
2 feed [fid] (v.) 餵養
3 mention [ˈmɛnʃən] (v.) 提及
4 discover [dɪsˈkʌvɚ] (v.) 發現
5 destroy [dɪˈstrɔɪ] (v.) 毀滅

Now it is Thursday 12th May, and the Sweeper is in the forest on the dusty red road. He gets back inside his Land Rover and makes a telephone call. He speaks to a man in an office, who simply says, "Good," and puts down the phone. Then the man in the office makes a call. He calls a number in England, and another man listens and he says: "Good. This did *not* happen. Make sure no one ever discovers[4] the true story. You understand?"

"I understand," says the man in the office in Africa, the man in a city called Abidjan in a small country called the Ivory Coast.

"If the real story got out, it could destroy[5] the company," says the man in England.

"No one will ever know the real story," says the man in Abidjan, looking out across the plateau[1], over the fringe[2] of high-rise buildings towards the lagoon[3]. "I've made sure of that."

"Good," says the man in England again. "There'll be a bonus[4] at the end of the year, I imagine." And he puts down the phone. He is not a man to use unnecessary words or continue to talk after he's said what he wants to say. He is a man who uses few words. But when he speaks, other men act.

---

## Secrets

- Have you ever had a secret?
- Has anyone ever told you a secret?
- When is it good to keep something secret? When is it bad?

---

\*     \*     \*     \*     \*     \*

And what about the second thing that happened on Thursday 12th May? That took place in a school in Cambridge, in England. It was the last class before lunch, and Tricia Johnson was presenting[5] a project[6] to her geography[7] class:

1 plateau [plæˈto] (n.) 高原
2 fringe [frɪndʒ] (n.) 邊緣
3 lagoon [ləˈgun] (n.) 潟湖
4 bonus [ˈbonəs] (n.) 獎金
5 present [prɪˈzɛnt] (v.) 做報告；發表
6 project [ˈprɑdʒɛkt] (n.) 方案；計畫
7 geography [ˈdʒɪˈɑgrəfɪ] (n.) 地理

"First, here are some facts:
1. Food in the UK now travels 50% further than it did 15 years ago.
2. Transportation[1] of food is responsible for 33% of the increase in road freight[2] over the last 15 years.
3. Here in the UK, road transport[3] is the only source of a greenhouse gas (carbon dioxide[4]) that's still increasing.

"I thought we could produce a leaflet[5]," she continued, "It'll tell people about the number of miles that their food travels to get to the supermarkets. We could give them these facts, and facts about the air miles that their food uses."

"Does that mean that cabbages get free flights to Spain?" asked Pete, the class joker[6].

No one answered him, though his gang of friends laughed.

"Let's compare two vegetables," said Tricia. "The first is in the supermarket down the road, and it's a packet of beans. It comes from Kenya and has traveled 4,333 miles to get here. The beans were picked five days ago and were sprayed[7] with chemicals[8] to stop them going brown on the journey[9]. They've been packed in plastic[10] and have traveled by road and air and road."

"They need a holiday in Spain," said Pete.

---

1 transportation [ˌtrænspəˈteʃən] (n.) 運輸
2 freight [fret] (n.) 貨運
3 transport [trænsˈpɔrt] (n.) 運送
4 carbon dioxide [ˈkɑrbən daɪˈɑksaɪd] 二氧化碳
5 leaflet [ˈliflɪt] (n.) 傳單
6 joker [ˈdʒokɚ] (n.) 愛耍寶的人

"The second vegetable is in the farmers' market which is on Midsummer Common[11] on Sundays. Here you have a paper bag with organic[12] carrots in it that have traveled six miles from the farm where they were picked the day before the market. They have been cleaned by being washed in the field, and they have never been sprayed with any chemicals."

Tricia sat down after she'd finished her presentation[13]. She knew it was good and she'd worked very hard to get all the information. Mrs Ashley, the geography teacher, was pleased. The class were impressed too and they agreed to raise the money to produce a leaflet, which they would hand out[14] outside the supermarket.

Then it happened. Just before lunch, after the bell. Tricia was putting all her books into her bag when Daniel Marsh came up to her. Daniel Marsh walked across the room to speak to Tricia Johnson.

Daniel Marsh, who was widely acknowledged[15] to be the coolest boy in the school. Daniel Marsh, who had almost-black hair and green eyes, and who played the guitar like Jimi Hendrix. The same Daniel Marsh who never talked to any of the girls in the class, although many of them dreamt of him at night.

---

7  spray [spre] (v.) 噴
8  chemical [`kɛmɪkl̩] (n.) 化學物品
9  journey [`dʒɜʒnɪ] (n.) 旅程
10  plastic [`plæstɪk] (n.) 塑膠
11  common [`kɑmən] (n.) 公共用地

12  organic [ɔrˋgænɪk] (a.) 有機的
13  presentation [ˏprɛznˋteʃən] (n.)
    做報告；報告
14  hand out 分送
15  acknowledge [əkˋnɑlɪdʒ] (v.) 承認

This was an unprecedented[1] moment. Tricia Johnson is not one of the prettier girls in the class. She's not as unattractive[2] as she thinks she is, but her hair is ordinary[3] and she's not as slim[4] as she wants to be. But Daniel Marsh, who was eighteen, and six months older than her, was talking to her. Daniel Marsh was talking about her project.

"That was so cool, Tricia," he said. "It's really important we put pressure[5] on the supermarkets."

Tricia smiled and nodded[6]. She couldn't say anything.

"There's something else I'd like to talk to you about," he said.

"Yeah?" said Tricia.

"Are you free to come over to my place later?"

Tricia nodded. Unless she was physically[7] restrained[8] or in hospital, she was going to be free to go over to Daniel Marsh's place. No one in her class had ever been invited back to Daniel's. Not since they'd all been children. Daniel Marsh had asked Tricia over. This was an event. And it was the second event of 12th May – and the event that started it all.

.

---

1 unprecedented [ʌnˈprɛsəˌdɛntɪd] (a.) 無先例的
2 unattractive [ˌʌnəˈtræktɪv] (a.) 無吸引力的
3 ordinary [ˈɔrdnˌɛrɪ] (a.) 普通的
4 slim [slɪm] (n.) 苗條的
5 pressure [ˈprɛʃɚ] (n.) 壓力
6 nod [nɑd] (v.) 點頭
7 physically [ˈfɪzɪklɪ] (adv.) 身體上地
8 restrain [rɪˈstren] (v.) 阻止；監禁
9 lean [lin] (v.) 靠
10 tip [tɪp] (v.) 使傾斜；傾倒
11 committee [kəˈmɪtɪ] (n.) 委員會

"What do you know about the carbon trade?" asked Daniel. He leaned[9] back, tipping[10] his chair. At home, Tricia's mother always complained when Tricia or her brother Nick did that, but Mrs Marsh didn't seem to mind. Indeed, Daniel's mother seemed different from Tricia's in many ways. She worked, while Tricia's mother didn't – though she was on several committees[11], which seemed to involve having people round and drinking a lot of coffee.

---

### Parents

- Do your parents ever complain to you about things you do?
- What do they expect you to do?

---

Mrs Marsh had always worked. Daniel's father had died when he was two and they needed the money. Tricia hadn't known about Daniel's father; Daniel told her on the way to his house.

"Just so you don't ask about him," he said.

"That's sad," she said, thinking no one at school knows anything about Daniel. We all like him, but he never talks about himself.

"Yeah. Mum still misses him. I never knew him, so there's nothing to miss. She's an architect[1], by the way."

"Who?" Tricia's mind had wandered[2].

"Mum," said Daniel.

"Oh," replied Tricia. "That's great," she added, thinking that was why she had never seen Daniel's mother. She wouldn't have time to do things with the other mums.

She imagined they would live in a new house, but they didn't. It was a typical Victorian terrace[3]; many of her friends lived in houses just like it. Tricia had always been conscious[4] that her own home was different from those of the other girls at school. It was bigger and, though it was new, it was built in a traditional style in red brick. It also had lots of columns[5] and a garage designed to look like a dovecot[6] and a huge gateway[7] with wrought-iron[8] gates that included her father's initials[9].

She had a feeling this was not the kind of house Daniel's mum would design. She felt that Daniel would laugh at the initials and the statues[10] of the lion and the unicorn[11] on top of the stone gateposts[12].

---

1 architect [ˈɑrkəˌtɛkt] (n.) 建築師
2 wander [ˈwɑndɚ] (v.) 漫遊
3 terrace [ˈtɛrəs] (n.) 露臺
4 conscious [ˈkɑnʃəs] (a.) 有意識到的
5 column [ˈkɑləm] (n.) 圓柱
6 dovecot [ˈdʌvˌkɑt] (n.) 鴿舍
7 gateway [ˈgetˌwe] (n.) 入口處
8 wrought-iron [ˌrɔtˈaɪən] (n.) 鍛鐵
9 initial [ɪˈnɪʃəl] (n.) 姓名的首字母
10 statue [ˈstætʃu] (n.) 雕像
11 unicorn [ˈjunɪˌkɔrn] (n.) 獨角獸
12 gatepost [ˈgetˌpost] (n.) 門柱

The outside of Daniel's house looked like all the other houses in the street. But inside the walls had been knocked down to create[13] one large open-plan[14] living space. This was painted red and was full of light from windows at both ends of the room. One wall was lined with books, and two guitar cases[15] leaned against the bookcase[16].

At the kitchen end was a large pine[17] table where she and Daniel were now sitting in a mess[18] of papers and magazines, some of which had cascaded[19] on to the floor. In the middle of the mess there was a computer where Daniel checked his emails the moment he came in.

Daniel's mother was cooking something with white wine, tomatoes and garlic, and seemed not to mind the chaos[20] created by her son. Tricia's mother always screamed[21] at her when she scattered[22] her papers all over the kitchen table.

Teresa Johnson liked everything to look nice all the time. Which meant constant[23] redecoration[24], new cushions, and new curtains, and a house that looked as if no one actually lived there. Tricia's friends always commented on how tidy[25] it was whenever they visited her and she had learned to read the subtext[26]: it wasn't natural.

---

13  create [krɪ`et] (v.) 創造；創作
14  open-plan [`opən`plæn] (a.) 開敞式平面佈置的
15  guitar case 吉他盒
16  bookcase [`bʊk͵kes] (n.) 書架
17  pine [paɪn] (n.) 松樹
18  mess [mɛs] (n.) 凌亂
19  cascade [kæs`ked] (v.) 瀑布似地落下

20  chaos [`keɑs] (n.) 混亂
21  scream [skrim] (v.) 尖叫
22  scatter [`skætɚ] (v.) 散佈
23  constant [`kɑnstənt] (a.) 不間斷的
24  redecoration [ri͵dɛkə`reʃən] (n.) 重新裝潢
25  tidy [`taɪdɪ] (a.) 整潔的
26  subtext [`sʌbtɛkst] (n.) 弦外之音

But it was how her mother liked it, so there wasn't anything she could do about it. Tricia felt more at home here, at Daniel's. His mum seemed more relaxed than hers.

## Relaxation

- Do you think that you are a relaxed person?
- What things do you find relaxing? What things agitate you?

It was two days since she had first gone home with him and started to talk about what they could do to stop global warming[1]. It was Saturday morning. Her parents were at the races with some clients[2]. Her mother had bought a new outfit[3] in London for the occasion[4], because her father's firm was sponsoring[5] the event[6], and she wanted to look her best, she said. So Tricia was free to spend the day at Daniel's. Mrs Johnson was delighted[7] that Tricia had a new friend and wasn't going to be hanging around[8] the house on her own.

Tricia was happy, too. She couldn't believe that her relationship with Daniel had developed so quickly. He'd even put his arm round her at school when they were walking down the corridor[9].

---

1 global warming 全球氣候暖化
2 client [ˋklaɪənt] (n.) 客戶
3 outfit [ˋaʊtˏfɪt] (n.) 全套裝備
4 occasion [əˋkeʒən] (n.) 場合
5 sponsor [ˋspɑnsɚ] (v.) 贊助
  (n.) 贊助人
6 event [ɪˋvɛnt] (n.) 活動
7 delighted [dɪˋlaɪtɪd] (a.) 高興的
8 hang around 閒蕩
9 corridor [ˋkɔrɪdɚ] (n.) 走廊

Tiffany, the blondest blonde[1] in the class had stopped and stared when she and Daniel had walked past. She didn't know that Daniel was discussing ways to get shoppers to buy more local foods – but Tricia didn't care. She was in love, and she had finally found someone who thought as she did. Life couldn't get much better than this. She tried to concentrate[2] on what he was saying.

"Well," said Daniel. He sat forward and tapped[3] at his keyboard. "What do you know about the carbon trade?"

Tricia searched her mind and found nothing.

"Okay," said Daniel. "What do you know about Kyoto?"

"Place in Japan," said Tricia. "It used to be the capital[4] city. Has lots of old temples[5] and shrines[6]."

"Very funny," said Daniel.

---

1  blonde [blɑnd] (n.) 白膚金髮碧眼的女孩
2  concentrate [ˋkɑnsɛnˏtret] (v.) 專注
3  tap [tæp] (v.) 輕敲
4  capital [ˋkæpətl̩] (a.) 首要的
5  temple [ˋtɛmpl̩] (n.) 寺廟
6  shrine [ʃraɪn] (n.) 聖壇；神殿

Tricia smiled. "Kyoto is the place where the world leaders met and signed an agreement[7] to stop climate change and reduce[8] greenhouse gases. Except the USA, who wouldn't sign it."

"More or less," said Daniel. "The Kyoto Protocol[9] was signed in 1997 by 180 countries, and called for[10] 38 industrialized[11] countries to reduce their greenhouse gas emissions[12]."

"Wow," laughed Tricia. "You're an expert[13]! And it's carbon dioxide that causes these gases."

"Yeah," agreed Daniel.

"But I still don't understand what the carbon trade is exactly," Tricia continued.

"Well," Daniel stopped tipping his chair and leaned forward. Tricia could almost feel his breath on her cheek, and his skin smelled of honey. She wanted to touch his face. She wanted him to kiss her. She tried to concentrate.

"The aim of Kyoto," said Daniel, "was to reduce greenhouse gases overall, but some countries obviously weren't going to meet the target[14], so instead of them getting penalties[15] for destroying the planet[16], they came up with a scheme[17]. This was the carbon trade. Basically it means that non-polluting countries and companies can sell their 'good carbon points' to companies in polluting countries, and in this way keep to a kind of global limit."

---

7 agreement [əˈgrimənt] (n.) 協定
8 reduce [rɪˈdjus] (v.) 減少
9 protocol [ˈprotəˌkɑl] (n.) 協議
10 call for 呼籲
11 industrialized [ɪnˈdʌstrɪəlaɪzd] (a.) 工業化的
12 emission [ɪˈmɪʃən] (n.) 釋放
13 expert [ˈɛkspɚt] (n.) 專家
14 target [ˈtɑrgɪt] (n.) 目標
15 penalty [ˈpɛnḷtɪ] (n.) 罰款
16 planet [ˈplænɪt] (n.) 行星
17 scheme [skim] (n.) 計畫；方案

"But doesn't that mean the rich countries can buy the right to go on chucking[1] carbon into the air?"

"Yup[2], it does. The idea was that if companies had to pay to go on polluting, they might cut back[3]. But it doesn't really work like that. They find ways round it. That's why Carban, our organization, is campaigning to ban[4] the carbon trade. We want companies to be forced to lower their emissions."

Tricia knew a bit now about Carban, the organization that Daniel did voluntary[5] work for in his spare[6] time.

---

### Spare Time

- What do you do in your spare time?
- Do you do voluntary work? What voluntary work would you like to do?

---

"You can find out a lot of this on the carbon trade watch website," Daniel told her. "There are lots of environmentalists[7] who are really worried about what's going on. Like money for reforesting[8] going on eucalyptus[9] plantations[10] that are then burned to make charcoal[11]. The idea's supposed to be that if you plant trees you create a 'carbon sink[12]' that absorbs[13] the carbon – but if you go and burn those trees for charcoal, you put more carbon into the air, not less."

1. chuck [tʃʌk] (v.) 嘔出
2. yup [jʌp] (adv.) 是啊（yes 的變體）
3. cut back 削減
4. ban [bæn] (v.) 禁止
5. voluntary [ˈvɑlənˌtɛrɪ] (a.) 自願的
6. spare [spɛr] (a.) 剩餘的；空閒的
7. environmentalist [ɪnˌvaɪrənˈmɛntlɪst] (n.) 環保人士
8. reforest [riˈfɔrɪst] (v.) 重新造林
9. eucalyptus [ˌjukəˈlɪptəs] (n.) 尤加利樹
10. plantation [plænˈteʃən] (n.) 人造林
11. charcoal [ˈtʃɑrˌkol] (n.) 木炭
12. sink [sɪŋk] (n.) 水槽
13. absorb [əbˈsɔrb] (v.) 吸收

"That's awful."

"It's happening all the time. The way things are going, the whole of the Amazon rainforest could become a desert within our lifetime . . ."

"But wouldn't that . . .?" Tricia began.

"Double the speed of global warming? Yeah. Make the planet uninhabitable[1]? Sure."

"But why don't governments do something?"

"Governments don't rule the world," said Daniel. "Global corporations[2] do. They have a vested interest[3] in keeping quiet. Though if things get any worse, I think maybe they will act. Or maybe I'm just more optimistic[4] than some campaigners[5] I know."

"This is so depressing," said Tricia.

"That's why we've got to do something," said Daniel. He tapped away on his keyboard, and then leant forward, frowning[6].

"What is it?" asked Tricia.

Daniel shook his head as he read an email. Then he made a few notes and deleted[7] it.

"What?" asked Tricia again.

"I'll tell you later," said Daniel quietly, indicating[8] his mother.

"So . . ." said Tricia, an hour or so later, when Mrs Marsh had gone to her study to work. "What was all that about?"

---

1 uninhabitable [ˌʌnɪnˈhæbɪtəbl̩] (a.) 不適於居住的
2 corporation [ˌkɔrpəˈreʃən] (n.) 股份公司
3 vested interest 既得利益
4 optimistic [ˌɑptəˈmɪstɪk] (a.) 樂觀的
5 campaigner [kæmˈpenɚ] (n.) 從事社會運動的人
6 frown [fraʊn] (v.) 皺眉
7 delete [dɪˈlit] (v.) 刪除
8 indicate [ˈɪndəˌket] (v.) 指出
9 offshoot [ˈɔfˌʃut] (n.) 分枝
10 investigate [ɪnˈvɛstəˌget] (v.) 調查
11 scam [skæm] (n.) 騙錢；陰謀
12 finance [faɪˈnæns] (v.) 提供資金
13 hack [hæk] (v.) 非法侵入
14 enquiry [ɪnˈkwaɪrɪ] (n.) 打聽

"I don't want Mum to know, because she'll worry," said Daniel. "But there's an offshoot[9] of Carban that's started to investigate[10] a huge new carbon-trade deal in Africa, and we're certain it's a scam[11]. And we think it's financed[12] by a British company, too, but we haven't found out who they are yet."

"Why would that make your Mum worry?" asked Tricia.

"A few reasons. Like the way we're getting the information might not be quite legal . . ."

"Hacking[13]?" asked Tricia.

Daniel nodded. "Though we did have a guy over in Africa making some enquiries[14], but he got some illness or other and had to come home. Or so he said. It's possible he was warned off[15]."

"Seriously?"

"Absolutely,[16]" said Daniel. "There are millions of pounds at stake[17] here. And these people will do anything to make sure their scam doesn't get found out. That's why I can't keep any records. It's not safe. And I definitely[18] don't want Mum to know. She'd go crazy if she thought what I was doing was dangerous."

---

## Danger

- Have you ever felt you were in danger?
- What would you do if you thought your friend was doing something dangerous?

---

15 warn off 警告不得靠近
16 absolutely [ˈæbsəˌlutlɪ] (adv.) 絕對地

17 at stake 在危急關頭
18 definitely [ˈdɛfənɪtlɪ] (adv.) 當然

Tricia looked round the comfy[1] kitchen. She couldn't imagine a safer place.

"Isn't that a bit – well – melodramatic[2]?" she asked.

"Maybe." Daniel laughed. "Anyhow, I make sure no one can trace[3] stuff[4] back to me."

"So what was the email about?" asked Tricia.

"It was about an informant[5], called Winston. He found out about us from our website and contacted[6] us. He said that there were things going on in his company that we ought to know about. We think he's going to tell us what's actually going on. He's a mineralogist[7]. Which asks the question: why does a company that says it's building a dam[8] need a mineralogist?"

"Is that what the company's doing?" Tricia asked. "Building a dam?"

"That's what they say," Daniel told her. "But it's in the middle of the Ivory Coast, which isn't exactly one of the easiest places to get information out of. If they really are building a hydro[9]-electric dam to make electricity for Abidjan – that's the biggest city – that's good. It's clean energy. Which is why the scheme's getting millions of dollars as a carbon sink. But there are things about this project that ring lots of alarm bells. And lots of people think it's not actually a carbon sink at all."

---

1 comfy [ˈkʌmfɪ] (a.) 舒適的
2 melodramatic [ˌmɛlədrəˈmætɪk] (a.) 情節劇似的
3 trace [tres] (v.) 追蹤
4 stuff [stʌf] (n.) 東西
5 informant [ɪnˈfɔrmənt] (n.) 告密者
6 contact [kənˈtækt] (v.) 聯絡
7 mineralogist [ˌmɪnəˈrælədʒɪst] (n.) 礦物學家
8 dam [dæm] (n.) 水壩
9 hydro- [ˈhaɪdro] (pref.) 水的
10 swarm [swɔrm] (v.) 被擠滿
11 nasty [ˈnæstɪ] (a.) 齷齪的
12 chunk [tʃʌŋk] (n.) 大塊
13 offshore [ˈɔfˈʃor] (a.) 境外的
14 account [əˈkaʊnt] (n.) 帳戶
15 untraceable [ʌnˈtresəbl̩] (a.) 難以追蹤的
16 source [sors] (n.) 來源
17 thriller [ˈθrɪlə] (n.) 驚悚小說

"What sort of things?" asked Tricia.

"Firstly, the company's swarming[10] with people who work for Afcob, which is a really nasty[11] mining company with a history of using child workers in mines in Congo and polluting chunks[12] of rainforest in Chad. And Afcob only really exists as a name, as it's owned by dozens of small companies with head offices in places that are famous for offshore[13] accounts[14] like the Bahamas and the Cayman Islands."

"Untraceable[15] sources[16]," said Tricia who had read enough thrillers[17] to know about offshore accounts.

"So what we're trying to find out is why they've chosen this bit of the river in the middle of the Ivory Coast. We want to know if they really are building a hydro-electric dam. The trouble is, the place is miles from anywhere and all the roads are guarded, so we can't find out what's going on."

"But what about the mineralogist?"

"Winston. Yeah. That's the nasty bit. He was going to tell us what was happening. He said he was very worried. Then a couple of days ago they sacked him. And now he's dead and the company says it's suicide[1]."

"That's awful!"

"Except it wasn't suicide. The villagers found his body in some bushes. Somebody shot him and they forgot to leave the gun behind."

Tricia's eyes ached[2]. It was two hours later and she was trying to find out about mining in the Ivory Coast. Most of the documents[3] she had been reading online had been in French, which she was studying for her A-level exam. But somehow mining language hadn't been a major feature of her studies, and she was finding it hard to understand.

It seemed that the Ivory Coast had everything – diamonds, gold, oil, gas. Yet it was also incredibly[4] poor, and most of the population survived[5] on what they could grow. And that seemed like a list from a geography lesson: cocoa, coffee, bananas, maize[6], pineapples.

"Did you know that the Ivory Coast once had the largest forests in West Africa?" she asked Daniel. "But there's hardly any forest left."

---

1 suicide [ˈsuə‚saɪd] (n.) 自殺
2 ache [ek] (v.) 持續性的疼痛
3 document [ˈdɑkjəmənt] (n.) 文件
4 incredibly [ɪnˈkrɛdəblɪ] (adv.) 難以置信地
5 survive [səˈvaɪv] (v.) 倖存
6 maize [mez] (n.) 〔英〕玉蜀黍

7 log [lɔg] (v.) 伐木
8 proper [ˈprɑpɚ] (a.) 適合的
9 semi- [ˈsɛmɪ] (pref.) 半的
10 embargo [ɪmˈbɑrgo] (n.) 禁止買賣
11 shrug [ʃrʌg] (v.) 聳肩
12 rebel [ˈrɛbl] (n.) 反抗者

"Logging[7]?" he asked.

"I think so. I don't know the proper[8] word in French, but I think that's what it says. But now, except for a bit that's a national park, it's all – what's the word in English? – I suppose we'd say 'semi[9]-desert'. That's terrible!" she added.

"But what about the mining?" asked Daniel.

"I'm getting there. This isn't easy. Most of the mines are controlled by a state-owned company. There's a lot about embargos[10] on diamonds from the Ivory Coast because they're being used to finance the fighting. Is there a war on there?"

Daniel shrugged[11]. "I don't think so. Maybe rebel[12] groups fighting the government. Mum might know – but she'd want to know why I wanted to know. What else?"

The thought crossed Tricia's mind that perhaps Daniel was asking her to help him just because she was studying French. She put the thought aside, though it continued to bother her. At least she was spending time with him, whereas Anthea, who was really beautiful, and was actually working as a model during the holidays, wasn't. And Anthea fancied[1] Daniel a lot, but he'd never asked her home for coffee.

Tricia had tried casually to mention Anthea's name the previous day.

"Can't stand girls like that," Daniel said. "Not a thought in their head. I get bored walking past them in the corridor."

Tricia laughed, though she felt a bit of a traitor[2]. Anthea was supposed to be a friend of hers, even though Tricia did feel that the friendship was always a bit one-sided[3]. Tricia helped Anthea with her homework and revision[4], and Anthea allowed Tricia to join her group at their table in the canteen[5].

## Friendship

- What qualities do you look for in a friend?
- Is loyalty important? Think of a time when you were loyal to a friend or when a friend was loyal to you.

Tricia sighed quietly and stopped asking herself whether Daniel really liked her, and started concentrating on the web pages. There was something about cobalt[6].

"Is cobalt something that's mined?" she asked.

Daniel almost leapt[7] across the table. "Too right it is! And it's incredibly valuable. You need it to make long-life batteries and radiation[8] and stuff. Everyone wants cobalt."

"Well, it seems there was a cobalt mine in the sixties in a place called Soubré, and for some reason they stopped mining it, but it doesn't say why."

"I need to ring someone," said Daniel.

"Who?" asked Tricia.

"John," said Daniel, "he's a friend of mine. I met him at a protest meeting last year. He teaches at the University of East Anglia and he's an expert on all this. He's a member of Carban too, so if anyone knows about the mine, it'll be John."

Tricia couldn't make out much from Daniel's end of the conversation, which was mostly "Yeah" and "Right" and "Really!"

But then Daniel said: "There's a website? That's amazing. What's the password? Hold on – I'll just write it down."

Tricia watched as he wrote down a string[9] of letters and numbers.

---

1 fancy ['fænsɪ] (v.) 喜愛
2 traitor ['tretɚ] (n.) 背叛者
3 one-sided ['wʌn'saɪdɪd] (a.) 片面的
4 revision [rɪ'vɪʒən] (n.) 修訂
5 canteen [kæn'tin] (n.) 學校的餐廳

6 cobalt ['kobɔlt] (n.) 鈷
7 leap [lip] (v.) 跳躍（動詞三態：leap; leaped/leapt; leaped/leapt）
8 radiation [ˌredɪ'eʃən] (n.) 放射能
9 string [strɪŋ] (n.) 一串

"What is it?" she asked after he put down the phone.

"He's given me a website to help me find out who's behind this. It belongs to a bank. John thinks they may be involved in financing some carbon schemes."

Daniel keyed in the numbers and began to read the text on the screen.

"What was the name of the place?" he asked.

"Soubré," replied Tricia. "It's on the Sassandra River."

"There's a map of a proposed[1] hydro-electric dam at Soubré," said Daniel. "It's a huge scheme. I'll print it out."

He gave it to Tricia. She frowned.

"That's really odd, because I've been reading about another huge international plan for a hydro-electric dam at Soubré, but it isn't in the same place as this. This . . ."

She looked at another map. "This is where the mine was."

"Two dams?" asked Daniel. "That doesn't make sense."

Tricia went back to her notes.

"Okay – there was a plan for a dam at Soubré years ago, but it wasn't built because of the damage it would cause to the local population and the nearby national park. Though there's a French company that's looking at it again. But that's here, north of Soubré."

Daniel looked at the map.

"And the dam that the bank's financing is south of Soubré," continued Tricia.

"Where the mine was," said Daniel.

"So why build a dam on the site of a mine?"

"I don't know," said Daniel. "I'll ask John."

Daniel rang his friend. This time he said even less, but nodded a lot.

"Well?" asked Tricia.

"John thinks it's a tailings[2] dam," said Daniel.

"What's that?" asked Tricia. "What's tailings?"

"Tailings is a name you give to all the stuff that's left over when you dig[3] copper[4] or silver or whatever out of the ground. In the old days, the way they mined was really wasteful[5]. They just went for the one thing they could see, and everything else just got piled up[6] around the mine or tipped[7] into water. They often used to dam a river to make a kind of deep pond where they could keep all this stuff. That's a tailings dam."

"So why build a new dam?" asked Tricia.

"The thing about tailings dams is that they're often full of stuff that's really valuable today."

"Like cobalt," said Tricia.

"Exactly," agreed Daniel. "And it's much cheaper to reprocess[8] the cobalt from the water than dig it out of the ground."

1 proposed [prə`pozd] (a.) 被提議的
2 tailing [`telɪŋ] (n.) 礦渣
3 dig [dɪg] (v.) 挖掘
4 copper [`kɑpɚ] (n.) 銅
5 wasteful [`westfəl] (a.) 造成破壞的
6 pile up 堆放起來
7 tip [tɪp] (v.) 傾倒
8 reprocess [ri`prɑsɛs] (v.) 再加工

"What's wrong with that?" asked Tricia.

"Well, it's not a way to save carbon," Daniel told her, "though the company seems to be getting money from the government as a carbon sink. So that's wrong. Plus, when they process the stuff in a tailings dam, it's really dangerous. John says there've been all kinds of disasters[1]. There was a case in Guyana where cyanide[2] got into the river. So it's not a good thing to do."

"But it could make a company a lot of money . . ." said Tricia.

"Millions," said Daniel. He returned to the computer and continued to read.

"Yes!" he shouted. "I think I've found the company that's behind it."

Tricia leant over his shoulder.

"What's it called?" she asked.

"Tricolas," said Daniel. He turned to Tricia. "Hey, are you okay? You've gone really white!"

"It's just something I ate," mumbled Tricia as she ran to the loo[3].

1 disaster [dɪ`zæstɚ] (n.) 災難
2 cyanide [`saɪə,naɪd] (n.) 氰化物
3 loo [lu] (n.) 廁所
4 distract [dɪ`strækt] (v.) 使分心
5 sparse [spɑrs] (a.) 貧乏的
6 ebony [`ɛbənɪ] (a.) 黑檀木製的
7 ancient [`enʃənt] (a.) 古老的
8 massive [`mæsɪv] (a.) 粗重的；大型的
9 metal [`mɛtl̩] (n.) 金屬
10 filing cabinet [`faɪlɪŋ `kæbənɪt] 檔案櫃
11 wooden [`wʊdn̩] (a.) 木製的

Tricia couldn't remember the last time she'd been in her father's study. It wasn't that the room was off-limits, but there had always been a general rule not to go in while he was working.

"Don't distract[4] your father," her mother would say. "We wouldn't have all these nice things if he didn't work so hard."

And because the door was always closed, and there was nothing very interesting inside, Tricia never went in there. But she opened the door and went in now. It was different from the rest of the house – sparser[5], less friendly. There was very little in it except for a computer on her father's ebony[6] desk – Tricia wondered what Daniel would say about that, what ancient[7] tree in what rainforest had been cut down to make this massive[8] piece of furniture.

There was also an ugly gray metal[9] filing cabinet[10]. Tricia remembered that her mother had once suggested that a wooden[11] filing cabinet would be prettier, but her father had laughed at the idea.

"It's a place to keep documents safe," he said. "Who cares what it looks like?"

Her mother had sighed, but had given in; the study was certainly off-limits[1] to her design team.

The most comfortable thing in the room was a huge black leather chair with a matching[2] footstool[3]. Other than that, the only decorative object was a huge glass paperweight[4] that her father had won as a prize for something, and which was so heavy that even now Tricia could hardly lift it.

Tricia's parents were going to be away all day at the races, and her brother Nick was at college in Cambridge, so Tricia knew she was safe. Even so, she found herself tiptoeing[5] into the study as if she didn't want the house to hear her go in.

She sat down at her father's desk and turned on his computer.

Tricolas. She'd known it was her father's company the moment Daniel had said the word. Her father had created the name from the names of her brother and herself: Tricia and Nicholas. Surely it wasn't her father behind all of this? It couldn't be!

There was a password. Of course, there was a password. Tricia tried to think what it could be. A number? Her parents' birthdays? Nick's and her birthdays? No, they would be too easy to discover. What did her father care about most?

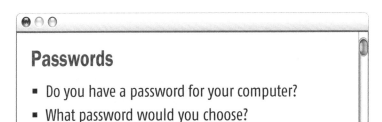

## Passwords

- Do you have a password for your computer?
- What password would you choose?

1 off-limits [ˈɔfˈlɪmɪts] (a.) 禁止進入的
2 matching [ˈmætʃɪŋ] (a.) 相配的
3 footstool [ˈfʊtˌstul] (n.) 腳凳
4 paperweight [ˈpepɚˌwet] (n.) 紙鎮
5 tiptoe [ˈtɪpˌto] (v.) 踮著腳走

Tricia sat back and looked round the room. There was a picture of her father with a group of politicians[1] in front of the House of Commons[2] and another one of her father in the winner's enclosure[3] at Newmarket racecourse[4]. He was pictured with the horse he'd owned with his partners[5].

Tricia remembered that he'd sold it straight after the race. He had made a good profit, her father had said. He'd been really pleased. As if a horse was just another thing to be traded, she thought, like the expensive wine he bought and never drank, and the drawings he got at auction[6], which he kept in the bank. The only pleasure her father had, it seemed, was in winning, in making more money.

Tricia's eyes wandered round the room until she found another picture of her father, this time on his yacht[7]. That was the only other thing he really enjoyed, she thought – racing his yacht. *The Peregrine[8] Falcon[9]*. A peregrine falcon? She suddenly smiled. Of course. The fastest falcon in the world, that kills as it flies.

Tricia typed in the word "peregrine." Yes. She was in.

The feeling of elation[10] passed in a second as she looked through the files. Tricolas. Soubré. They were all there. She could open them up and find all the information that Daniel needed. But then what? Could she actually give the information to Daniel and betray her father? And what would happen if she didn't? How many people would die if the dam was built?

---

1 politician [ˌpɑləˈtɪʃən] (n.) 政治家
2 House of Commons〔英〕下議院
3 enclosure [ɪnˈkloʒɚ] (n.) 圍場
4 racecourse [ˈresˌkors] (n.) 賽馬場
5 partner [ˈpɑrtnɚ] (n.) 夥伴
6 auction [ˈɔkʃən] (n.) 拍賣
7 yacht [jɑt] (n.) 遊艇；快艇
8 peregrine [ˈpɛrəgrɪn] (n.)〔鳥〕遊隼

Tricia knew that, in any case, she had to know everything. And she began to read.

It was all there – the mining report, the details on how they would reprocess the water in the tailings dam. "A sink of dirty red water worth millions" was how one report described it. Instead of a carbon sink collecting carbon so that the planet could breathe, you had a reservoir[11] of toxic[12] water that would make a few people very rich and could kill thousands.

The plan, it seemed was to build a new dam and use the electricity from this to process the water from the mine and filter[13] this water back into the river. There was a file about a report from a local specialist[14] – Tricia wondered if this was Winston. The file said that the specialist was worried. He thought that there was a risk from dangerous chemicals in the water such as arsenic[15] and cyanide. He told the company the work on the tailings dam could release[16] the chemicals into the Sassandra River and people would die.

What date was this? Just four days ago. Tricia looked to see if there was any recent reply. After an hour she found it. In a different folder[17] called "Jobs." It was an order for someone called the Sweeper to deal with a small internal[18] matter. The matter was called Winston.

---

9  falcon [ˈfɔlkən] (n.) 隼；獵鷹
10  elation [ɪˈleʃən] (n.) 得意洋洋
11  reservoir [ˈrɛzəˌvɔr] (n.) 貯水池
12  toxic [ˈtɑksɪk] (a.) 有毒的
13  filter [ˈfɪltə] (v.) 過濾

14  specialist [ˈspɛʃəlɪst] (n.) 專家
15  arsenic [ˈɑrsn̩ɪk] (n.) 砷；砒霜
16  release [rɪˈlis] (v.) 釋放出
17  folder [ˈfoldə] (n.) 檔案夾
18  internal [ɪnˈtɜnl̩] (a.) 內部的

"I know that you will carry out this job in the usual way," her father had written. "You all know that we can never release this information. The effect[1] on the company would be catastrophic[2]. The source of this information must be permanently[3] closed."

A sudden noise made Tricia jump. Someone was in the house. She was not alone.

Tricia copied all the important files onto her memory stick[4] and closed all the folders. She wondered if her father would notice that someone had opened the files. Why would he? It was his home computer. No one else but him ever used it.

Tricia turned off the computer. She crept[5] out of the study and into the hall.

"Hello!" she called, trying not to sound scared[6].

"Tricia!" called her brother. "Is that you, sis[7]? I thought someone must be at home because the alarm wasn't on. But the house was so quiet I thought you must be asleep."

"Just reading," she said.

She went into the kitchen where her brother was making himself coffee.

"What are you doing here?" she asked him. "I thought you were at college doing your exams."

1　effect [ɪˋfɛkt] (n.) 作用
2　catastrophic [ˌkætəˋstrɑkfɪk] (a.) 災難的
3　permanently [ˋpɝmənəntlɪ] (adv.) 永久地
4　memory stick 隨身碟
5　creep [krip] (v.) 躡手躡足地走 ( 動詞三態：creep; crept/creeped; crept/creeped )
6　scared [skɛrd] (a.) 驚嚇的
7　sis [sɪs] (n.) 〔口〕妹妹
8　rugby [ˋrʌgbɪ] (n.) 英式橄欖球
9　rubbish [ˋrʌbɪʃ] (n.) 垃圾；廢物
10　punch [pʌntʃ] (v.) 用拳猛擊
11　be fond of sb 喜歡某人
12　boarding school 寄宿學校
13　refuse [rɪˋfjuz] (v.) 拒絕

"I'm having a day off," Nick explained. "Rugby[8] match. Rubbish[9] it was, too. They couldn't hold on to a ball if it was made of glue.

Hey . . ." he stopped. "What's the matter, sis?"

Tricia realized her eyes were red from crying.

"Who is he?" Nick asked. "What's he done to you? Do you want me to punch[10] him?"

Tricia smiled. Although they weren't close, she was fond of[11] her brother. They had always been different, but ever since he'd gone to boarding school[12] and she'd insisted on going to the local high school, it seemed that they lived on different planets. It was boarding school that had changed Nick, and she didn't like the way he had changed. That was the reason that she'd refused[13] to go to boarding school herself.

She didn't want to become like Nick, with all his rich friends. All they talked about was where they were going to go skiing[1] in the winter and sailing in the summer. Tricia hated skiing and was seasick[2] on the yacht. Her ideal holiday was lying on the beach with some friends and swimming. She and Nick had very little in common. But he was still her brother.

"Nick," Tricia began, "can I trust you?"

"What kind of question's that? I'm your brother."

"I know. It's just that I don't know what to do. Listen, what would you do if you found out that Dad was involved[3] in something really bad?"

"Is this one of those stupid questionnaires[4] . . .?"

"No. I'm serious. I'm talking really bad. Illegal[5]."

"What are you on about[6]?" asked her brother, pouring milk into his coffee. "Dad's not like that."

"But if he was."

"Tricia. You're going to have to tell me what you're on about."

Tricia told him. She told him about the carbon trade, about the scam, about the tailings dam and about Winston. She told him everything. Almost everything. She didn't mention that she had copied all of this onto the memory stick that was in her pocket.

"You can't prove that Dad meant them to kill that guy," said Nick. "Not from those words. It wouldn't stand up in court[7]."

"This isn't a court," said Tricia. "This is you and me sitting round the kitchen table."

---

1 go skiing 去溜冰
2 seasick [`si,sik] (a.) 暈船的
3 involved [ɪn`vɑlvd] (a.) 牽扯在內的
4 questionnaire [,kwɛstʃən`ɛr] (n.) 問卷
5 illegal [ɪ`lig!] (a.) 非法的

"Exactly," said Nick. "And that's where it's got to stay. All that information you read on Dad's computer must never leave this house. Do you realize that?" he added. "It would destroy Dad if anyone found out."

## Family

- If you found out one of your family was involved in something illegal or bad what would you do?
- Do you think family members should cover up[8] for each other? Or do you think you would tell someone about what was happening?

"I know. That's why I was so upset[9]."

"Yeah." Nick looked pale[10] himself. "It's not a nice thing to find out. This friend of yours, what's his name?"

"Daniel," said Tricia.

"Daniel. Is he your boyfriend?"

"Sort of[11]" Tricia replied. She felt herself blushing[12]. "Daniel Marsh. He's really nice."

"Well, you have to make sure this Daniel Marsh guy never ever finds out that Tricolas is Dad's company. You don't think he suspected[13] anything?"

---

6 What are you on about? 你這是什麼意思？
7 court [kort] (n.) 法院
8 cover up 掩蓋
9 upset [ʌpˋsɛt] (a.) 心煩的；難過的
10 pale [pel] (a.) 蒼白的
11 sort of 有那麼一點兒
12 blush [blʌʃ] (v.) 臉紅
13 suspect [səˋspɛkt] (v.) 懷疑

"No," said Tricia. "I didn't say anything."

"Right," said Nick. "Now, promise me you won't tell Daniel."

"Okay," said Tricia slowly. She didn't think she was doing the right thing – but how could she betray[1] her own father?

"And Nick," she added, "you have to promise me not to tell Dad. He mustn't know I know."

"Of course I won't," said Nick. "He must never know that either of us know anything about this."

Tricia began to relax.

"Look, why don't you do something to take your mind off all this?" said Nick. "Go to a movie or something. Go and do girly[2] things with your friends."

"Girly things?" said Tricia. "What, like talking about makeup[3] or shoes? I don't do that."

"Well, do whatever you do do," said Nick. "Just try and forget all about this. It's not something we've really got any right to know about. It's Dad's world. Not ours."

Nick was probably right, thought Tricia as she sat on her bed staring at Camus'[4] *The Outsider*[5], which she ought to have been reading for her French class. She felt she should say something to Daniel. But that meant lying to him, and she knew that would be really hard. She hated lying, and wasn't any good at it. Daniel'd know straight away. Which meant she shouldn't see him. But how could she avoid seeing him unless she stopped going to school? It was all impossible. And in any case, not seeing Daniel was the worst thing she could imagine.

---

1  betray [bɪˈtre] (v.) 背叛
2  girly [ˈgɜˈlɪ] (a.) 女孩的
3  makeup [ˈmekˌʌp] (n.) 化妝品
4  Camus 法國存在主義作家卡繆（Albert Camus, 1913-60）
5  outsider [ˈautˈsaɪdɚ] (n.) 局外人

Martin Johnson was in a very bad mood[6]. He was losing money, and while the money part of this was irritating[7], the losing part was much worse. Martin did not like losing. What made it even more annoying was that while his horses continued to behave like seaside donkeys, the horses his wife bet[8] on won.

Race after race. Which Teresa thought was very amusing, as she only chose them for their names or because they reminded her of a holiday or even a dog she'd once known. And he actually knew something about horses.

He glared[9] at his wife, who laughed and waved a handful of notes[10] at him. He had to admit that Teresa looked good. She was high maintenance[11], always buying clothes and trips to the spa. And how could anyone need a handbag that cost £2,000, he wondered. But the clients liked her, and even after two children she looked much the same as she had when he'd married her.

His mobile phone[12] rang.

"Yes," he said, abruptly.

"Dad – it's Nick."

"Yeah, what do you want? I'm with people."

"Can anyone hear your conversation?" asked Nick.

6 mood [mud] (n.) 心情；情緒
7 irritating [ˈɪrəˌtetɪŋ] (a.) 令人感到煩躁的
8 bet [bɛt] (v.) 打賭
9 glare [glɛr] (v.) 怒視
10 note [not] (n.) 紙鈔
11 maintenance [ˈmentənəns] (n.) 生活費
12 mobile phone 手機

Martin walked towards the window of the sponsor's suite[1] that had cost him a small fortune.

"No," he said. "What's going on?"

"It's Tricia," said Nick. "She and a friend have found out about Tricolas."

"What are you on about?" asked Martin, feeling his blood go cold despite the warm day and his three-piece suit.

"The dam in Africa. Everything. The guy who died," his son told him.

"How?" asked his father.

"She read your files."

1 suite [swit] (n.) 一組（傢俱）
2 manage to 想辦法做到
3 dig up 挖出來

"She did what?" Martin realized he was shouting. Teresa was looking in his direction. He lowered his voice. "Why?" he asked Nick. "What was she doing?"

"She was doing some environmental thing with some guy from school, a boy called Daniel Marsh. He managed to[2] dig up[3] the stuff about Africa, and the name Tricolas came up. Tricia knew it was your company. So she read your files."

"The stupid girl! What's she going to do with the information?"

"Nothing," said Nick. "She's upset, you can imagine. But she promised me she wouldn't tell her boyfriend. She's just sitting at home."

"Good thing you were there. But why were you there? Why weren't you at college?"

"I just happened to come home. I was at a match."

."Just as well." Martin imagined what would happen if his files were put onto the Internet. It would be the end.

"I had to tell you, Dad."

"Course you did, Nick my boy. You did the right thing."

"But don't let Tricia know that you know. I promised her I wouldn't tell you. So you don't know," said Nick.

"I understand," said his father.

"You didn't order people to kill that man in Africa, did you?" Nick asked, suddenly sounding much younger.

"Course not. Just pay him off[1]. But he was a strange guy. I think he owed the wrong people money. You know what it's like out there. They're all fighting each other. His death wasn't anything to do with me. You couldn't think that."

"Of course not, Dad."

"Okay, good. So when are your mother and I going to see you?" asked his father, sounding happier. "Let's go and celebrate your end of term in style. Weekend in Paris, stay at the Ritz. Choose some chums[2]."

Martin excused himself from his clients and found a quiet corridor where he could make some phone calls without being heard. Within two minutes he had an address. He dialed another number.

"Is the Sweeper in town?" he asked. "Good. I've got another job for him."

"A small gas leak³?" Martin looked out at the racetrack⁴, but he couldn't see any horses. All he could see was a circle of dark water surrounded by trees, water that contained⁵ enough minerals⁶ to make an entire country rich. Dark water that was red from the minerals within it. His dream. His future.

"A small gas leak is an excellent idea," he said. "Collateral⁷ damage?" He thought for a second. "It's always sad when people die, but these things happen. Tell the Sweeper the most important thing is that I get the computer and no one knows it was stolen. He knows what to do. And," he added, "time is very important. Tell the Sweeper that if I get the computer tomorrow the bonus will be doubled."

He listened for a moment. "Yes," said Martin. "Good."

He looked down at the horses racing in front of him. The crowd was cheering⁸. He felt a thousand miles away. But he must play the game. He must go back to his clients and smile and make jokes. He took a deep breath and put a smile on his face.

"So who's the winner this time?" he asked. "Godfrey? Well done, old chap⁹! Another glass of champers¹⁰, I think."

He clicked his fingers at the waitress, who hurried over. Martin didn't even see her. He was an actor asleep on the stage. He knew the right words and actions, but he wasn't there. He was thinking about his daughter. Tricia. What was he going to do about her?

---

1 pay sb off 收買某人
2 chum [tʃʌm] (n.) 摯友
3 leak [lik] (n.) 滲漏
4 racetrack [ˋrestræk] (n.) 跑道
5 contain [kənˋten] (v.) 包含
6 mineral [ˋmɪnərəl] (n.) 礦物
7 collateral [kəˋlætərəl] (a.) 間接的
8 cheer [tʃɪr] (v.) 歡呼
9 chap [tʃæp] (n.) 傢伙
10 champers [ˋʃæmpɚz] (n.) 香檳
　( = champagne )

Tricia was very quiet on Sunday morning, but her mother didn't notice anything. She had a headache – that was the trouble with champagne[1]. She decided to spend the morning in bed. Tricia's father was in his study, and the door was shut. Nick was back at college.

After breakfast, Tricia sat in her room looking at her computer. She wanted to ring Daniel or email him. He'd sent her several text messages[2]. He sounded worried. It was so unfair; she wanted to see Daniel so much, but what could she say?

She pounded[3] her pillow. "Daniel! Why's this happening to us? Why's everything so difficult?" It was no good. She had to see him.

Tricia was walking down Mill Road when she heard the explosion[4]. She started to run towards Mawson Road, where Daniel lived. The police were trying to keep people out, but Tricia managed to get through[5] the barrier[6]. She was just turning the corner into Mawson Road when someone grabbed[7] her round the waist and pulled her behind a hedge[8]. It was Daniel. His face was red with crying.

"Daniel . . ." began Tricia.

"They killed Mum. She was in the house."

"What?"

1 champagne [ʃæmˋpen] (n.) 香檳
2 text message 手機簡訊
3 pound [paʊnd] (v.) 打；重擊
4 explosion [ɪkˋsploʒən] (n.) 爆炸
5 get through 通過
6 barrier [ˋbærɪr] (n.) 障礙物
7 grab [græb] (v.) 抓住
8 hedge [hɛdʒ] (n.) 樹籬

"I went out to get some bread and things for lunch and she was at home. And then just as I was coming back it just blew up[1]. The whole house. It's on the news already. They are saying it was a gas leak."

"I don't understand," said Tricia.

"How did they know?" asked Daniel.

"I don't know," said Tricia. Her father? she wondered, but Nick had promised not to say anything. But her father – he couldn't do that, could he? Blow up Daniel's house? Kill his mother?

"Maybe they were listening to John's calls," said Daniel.

"We need to get away," said Tricia. "They need to think you're dead, too. You have to disappear."

"How?" asked Daniel. "Where?"

"I don't know," said Tricia.

"We need a car, "said Daniel. "They have security[2] cameras[3] at all the bus and train stations."

"Nick's car's at home," said Tricia. "He doesn't need it during the term[4]. We can take it. Can you drive?"

"Yes; I passed my test last month – but where can we go?" Daniel asked.

"Give me a moment to think," said Tricia. "Stay here behind this hedge."

She looked at the house. There was no one there. "This place looks safe for the moment. I'll go and get Nick's car and pick you up."

---

1  blow up 炸毀
2  security [sɪˈkjʊrətɪ] (n.) 安全；保全
3  security camera 監視器
4  term [tɜm] (n.) 學期
5  drawer [ˈdrɔɚ] (n.) 抽屜
6  responsible [rɪˈspɑnsəbl̩] (a.) 負責任的
7  license [ˈlaɪsn̩s] (n.) 執照
8  ring road〔英〕外環道

The house was quiet, and Tricia quickly found Nick's keys in a drawer[5] in the hall. She was just about to go to her room when her father's study door opened and he walked out.

"Tricia, is that you? How's life?" he began.

Tricia didn't answer but pushed past him into his study. She didn't know how he knew about Daniel, but she suddenly had a feeling that her father was responsible[6].

"Was it you?" she asked. "Do you know that Daniel's mother is dead?"

"What are you talking about . . . ?" began her father, but then Tricia saw it. Daniel's computer, on her father's desk.

"No!" she screamed. "No! How could you?"

"Tricia! Stop!" her father shouted.

Tricia ran outside and jumped into Nick's car. Her father ran after her, but she took no notice and started the car. Nick had taught her on holiday and she knew how to drive even though she didn't have a license[7].

She drove very carefully, very slowly, to where Daniel was waiting for her. He got into the driving seat and drove towards the ring road[8].

"Where are we going?" he asked. "Why are we doing this? I don't know what I'm doing any more."

"We need to go somewhere safe just for a day or two until we work out what to do," said Tricia. "There's something I have to tell you. I know who owns Tricolas and who killed Winston and who blew up your house. My father!"

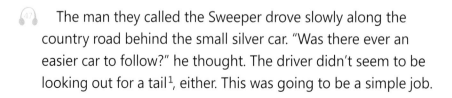 The man they called the Sweeper drove slowly along the country road behind the small silver car. "Was there ever an easier car to follow?" he thought. The driver didn't seem to be looking out for a tail[1], either. This was going to be a simple job.

1 tail [tel] (n.) 跟蹤者
2 grief [grif] (n.) 悲傷

The Sweeper was a man who liked things to be done properly. The explosion had gone well, but the boy hadn't been in the house, he'd discovered. He had watched from a window in a house along the road. And it was the boy who'd got the information. This would mean another accident, but it could be made to look like grief[2] – a suicide following the death of his mother. He didn't know who the girl was, but her presence wasn't a problem. Two deaths were as easy as one.

He drove slowly, reading the map and making plans..

Martin Johnson was worried. "You think he's going to finish the job?" he asked.

The man on the other end of the phone seemed to think that this was the case.

"No, it's not what I want," said Martin. "Can't you contact him?"

"No," the man told him. "The Sweeper only makes contact after he finishes a job. That makes it safer for everyone."

"You have to stop him," shouted Martin. "The boy he's chasing[1] is almost certainly driving my son's car. And my daughter's in the car. I've sent a killer after my own daughter!"

Martin stopped. He heard a noise outside his study. He went to look. It was his wife, Teresa; she'd heard the conversation from the hall and had fainted[2]. He ended his call, then picked his wife up[3] and carried[4] her into the sitting room[5].

"You heard?" he asked when she regained[6] consciousness[7].

"I never wanted to know," she said. "There was so much money. Too much money. I didn't ask any questions." She stared at her husband and her eyes were cold. "I trusted you," she said. "I never asked questions because I trusted you."

"I'll deal with it," said Martin. "I'll stop him. I won't let anything happen to Tricia."

"You say that Daniel Marsh has abducted[8] your daughter," said the detective[9], slowly. He was very careful with his words.

Martin Johnson was a close friend of the chief[10] superintendent[11]. He gave a lot of money to police charities[12]. He was a powerful man.

---

1 chase [tʃes] (v.) 追逐
2 faint [fent] (v.) 昏厥；暈倒
3 pick sb up 扶起某人
4 carry [ˈkærɪ] (v.) 攜帶
5 sitting room 起居室
6 regain [rɪˈgen] (v.) 恢復
7 consciousness [ˈkɑnʃəsnɪs] (n.) 意識
8 abduct [əbˈdʌkt] (v.) 綁架
9 detective [dɪˈtɛktɪv] (n.) 偵探
10 chief [tʃif] (a.) 主要的；等級最高的

"I think he may have been responsible for the explosion in Mawson Road," said Martin. "My daughter said he was interested in bomb-making equipment[13]. I believe he was part of some organization. My daughter said she didn't want to see him again. But he came round and stole my son's car and abducted my daughter. She's only 17, and I'm very worried about her. I think she's in serious danger."

The news about Tricia's abduction was broadcast[14] immediately. Everyone began to look for silver cars, and many couples were stopped and questioned.

Nick heard about it from a friend.

"Isn't that your sister?" his friend asked.

Nick rang his home and spoke to his mother. They talked quietly together and then Nick went to the nearest police station and made a long statement[15].

"That's very interesting," said the inspector[16]. "It also confirms[17] what Mrs Marsh has told us."

"But I thought she died in the explosion," said Nick.

"Luckily, she was in the garden," said the inspector. "She was knocked unconscious, but she seems to be fine."

"But what about my sister?" asked Nick.

"That is extremely[18] serious," agreed the inspector. "We've got every available police officer looking for your sister. But I'm afraid it's a question of whether we can find her in time."

---

11 superintendent [ˌsupərɪnˈtɛndənt] (n.) 〔英〕警司；警察督察長
12 charity [ˈtʃærətɪ] (n.) 慈善
13 equipment [ɪˈkwɪpmənt] (n.) 裝備
14 broadcast [ˈbrɔdˌkæst] (v.) 廣播
15 statement [ˈstetmənt] (n.) 供述
16 inspector [ɪnˈspɛktɚ] (n.) 調查員；督察
17 confirm [kənˈfɜm] (v.) 證實
18 extremely [ɪkˈstrimlɪ] (adv.) 極度地

Daniel and Tricia heard it on the news on the car radio.

"The police are hunting a suspected[1] terrorist[2], who they believe may be behind this morning's explosion in Cambridge. His name has not yet been released, but it is thought that he may have abducted the Cambridge teenager Tricia Johnson. The public should get in touch with the police immediately if they see a silver car with the registration number[3] . . ."

Tricia switched it off[4]. "Abducted?"

"That's your father," said Daniel. "He's been talking to the police."

"What are we going to do?" asked Tricia.

Daniel stopped the car. The road stretched[5] ahead of them, flat and straight. Parallel[6] to the road was a deep canal[7], and all around them were fields of dark fen[8] mud with rows of green vegetables. There was not a house to be seen in any direction. It was a sad and lonely place.

"If they think I'm a terrorist, they're going to shoot first and ask questions afterwards," Daniel said slowly.

"Not if I'm with you," said Tricia. "They won't shoot[9] me. And I've got the evidence[10] on my memory stick. We *will* get out of this."

"I don't know that I even care," said Daniel. "I keep thinking about Mum."

A small black car drove up and stopped beside them and a man got out. He was tall with gray hair and had dark glasses that covered half his face. Also, he was carrying a gun.

The Sweeper pointed the gun at Daniel as he got into the back of their car.

1 suspected [sə`spɛktɪd] (a.) 有嫌疑的
2 terrorist [`tɛrərɪst] (n.) 恐怖分子
3 registration number 汽車牌照號碼
4 switch off 關
5 stretch [strɛtʃ] (v.) 延伸
6 parallel [`pærə,lɛl] (a.) 平行的
7 canal [kə`næl] (n.) 運河
8 fen [fɛn] (n.) 沼澤
9 shoot [ʃut] (v.) 射殺（動詞三態：shoot; shot ; shot
10 evidence [`ɛvədəns] (n.) 證據

"This is a good place," said the Sweeper. "You've done my work for me." He pointed the gun at Tricia.

"Drive into the canal," he told Daniel, "or I shoot."

"We won't talk," said Daniel. "Please don't kill her."

"I don't want to shoot," said the Sweeper. "An accident's easier – but I'll shoot if necessary."

"Just like you shot Winston," said Tricia.

"You stupid children" said the Sweeper. "Why did you go and ask so many questions? Now, drive," he said.

Daniel put the car into first gear[1] and drove slowly off the road and straight into the canal.

Tricia was more scared than she'd ever been in her life. The water was rising fast. The Sweeper had jumped out of the car as it had left the road, but the water was pressing[2] against the doors and she and Daniel couldn't open them.

"Can you smash[3] the window?" asked Daniel.

Tricia tried to hit it with her shoe.

"It's too strong," she said. "It won't break!"

1 gear [gɪr] (n.) 汽車排檔
2 press [prɛs] (v.) 壓
3 smash [smæʃ] (v.) 打碎

Nick sat in the police car on his way home as the policeman talked on his mobile phone.

"A farmer has seen a silver car like yours up near the bird sanctuary[1]. We've sent a police helicopter[2]."

"Is it Tricia?" asked Nick. "This is all my fault," he said. "I trusted Dad."

"You're not responsible for your father," said the policeman. "You did the right thing."

"But if I'm too late?" asked Nick. "Oh, Tricia!"

1 sanctuary [ˈsæŋktʃʊˌɛrɪ] (n.) 鳥獸禁獵區；保護區
2 helicopter [ˈhɛlɪˌkɑptɚ] (n.) 直升機

There was almost no air in the car, and the water rose and rose.

"I'm so sorry," said Tricia.

"It's okay," said Daniel. "You didn't know."

"I love you," said Tricia. "*I'm going to die*", she thought, "*so I can say it at last.*"

Daniel took her hand. "Don't talk," he said. "We need to save the air."

Tricia pushed his head up. "I'm good at swimming underwater³," she said.

Then everything went black. So she didn't see the shadow pass overhead⁴ or hear the noise of the helicopter as it landed.

---

3 underwater [ˌʌndəˈwɔtə] (adv.) 在水面下
4 overhead [ˈovəhɛd] (adv.) 在頭頂上

## IX

Martin Johnson was sitting in the police station writing his statement when the superintendent returned.

"We've found your daughter," he said.

"Is she . . . ?" Martin couldn't finish the sentence.

"Alive? Yes," said the superintendent. "We got there just in time," he said. "A minute later, and your daughter and her friend would've been dead."

Martin Johnson put his head in his hands and wept.

"We have also arrested[1] a man that I think you know as the Sweeper. It seems police in at least seven countries want to talk to him. We've arrested him for causing an explosion and attempted[2] murder[3], but there are many other murder charges[4] against him. I believe *you* may be able to help us with some of those," he added.

---

1 arrest [əˋrɛst] (v.) 逮捕
2 attempted [əˋtɛmptɪd] (a.) 未遂的
3 murder [ˋmɝdɚ] (n.) 謀殺
4 charge [tʃɑrdʒ] (n.) 控訴

Tricia had a great many visitors in hospital. Nick and her mother were there every day, and Daniel and his mother came most days, too.

Daniel was a national[5] hero, and his picture was in every newspaper.

"There are all these phone calls," said his mother. "Television people who want to interview[6] him." She laughed. "He hates it! And the mail. Sacks of it. It's quite crazy."

Tricia tried to smile. Daniel was being very nice, but things weren't easy. It was *her* father who had tried to kill him and his mother. It was because of *her* telling Nick that they'd almost died.

None of this was in the papers, but there was a lot about her father. He was in prison now, and there were police at the door of her hospital ward[7] to protect her from the media[8]. The information she'd copied onto her memory stick was vital, as her father had destroyed his own computer records.

"They think you're a hero, too," continued Mrs Marsh. "You had an impossible choice."

"But it was my fault," said Tricia. "I told Nick."

---

5 national [ˈnæʃən!] (a.) 全國的
6 interview [ˈɪntəˌvju] (v.) 訪問
7 ward [wɔrd] (n.) 病房
8 media [ˈmidɪə] (n.) 媒體（medium 的複數）

"He's your brother," said Mrs Marsh. "You trusted him. And he did go to the police in the end. He saved you."

"Yeah," said Tricia.

She remembered the moments in the car. When she'd thought she'd been dying, she'd been happy. Daniel loved her and she loved him. But now everything was much harder.

"You're alive," said Mrs Marsh. "And so am I, and so is Daniel. And you'll be getting some really wicked[1] people sent to prison. Just think about that."

"Thanks," said Tricia. Mrs Marsh understood her very well.

"Daniel and you will be going to university soon," said Mrs Marsh. "Things will change."

## Change

- Think of a time when your life changed. What happened?
- What was life like before and after the change?

And so many things did change. Tricia thought that it was her mother who surprised her most.

"I used to be a really good secretary before I met your father," she said.

---

1 wicked [ˋwɪkɪd] (a.) 壞的；缺德的

All Martin Johnson's money had gone, and Tricia and her mother had moved to a small flat[1] on the other side of Cambridge. Teresa had got herself a job and, strangely, seemed much happier. And Nick had decided that he had nothing in common with all his old friends and had started to study seriously and look for a job, too.

Daniel had left school and was doing his exams at a private[2] college where the press[3] couldn't bother him. He had a job, too, presenting a program on television about climate change. He emailed Tricia, but she learned more about him from magazines than from him himself; he was about to go to the Arctic with a very beautiful meteorologist[4] she read. Life went on; she had exams the next day.

She opened up her book to study when a text message beeped[5] in on her mobile.

GOOD LUCK 2MORO
LOVE DANIEL

He hadn't forgotten her. Yes, life was good.

---

1 flat [flæt] (n.) 〔英〕公寓
2 private [`praɪvɪt] (a.) 私立的
3 press [prɛs] (n.) 新聞界;媒體
4 meteorologist [ˌmitɪə`rɑlədʒɪst] (n.) 氣象學者
5 beep [bip] (v.) 發短促尖銳的嗶嗶聲

## AFTER READING

## Ⓐ Characters

**1** Listen to the dialogues. Who are the characters talking about? Number the pictures.

**2** Which adjectives describe Martin Johnson? Circle them.

ambitious    brave    weak    powerful    creative
greedy    kind    cold-hearted    thoughtful    secretive

**3** Now fill in a fact file about Tricia's father.

| | |
|---|---|
| Name | |
| Nationality | |
| Personality | |
| Business | |
| Likes | |
| Dislikes | |

**4** Write the names of the characters beside the sentences.

- a He was a mineralogist and he was murdered.

- b He donates money to police charities.

- c She is campaigning to get people to buy local fruit and vegetables.

- d Her husband died and she works as an architect.

- e He buys silence with fear.

- f He is a student at Tricia's school and he is a member of Carban.

**5** The police want information about the Sweeper. What can you tell them about him? Answer the questions.

Police   What does he look like?
You
Police   Why is he called the Sweeper?
You
Police   In how many countries is he wanted by the police?
You
Police   How did he kill Winston?
You
Police   How did he attempt to kill Daniel the first time?
You
Police   And the second time?
You
Police   That's all for now. Thank you for your time. If we need to ask you any further questions, we'll contact you.

**6** Imagine you are a police officer. What questions would you ask Martin Johnson? Ask and answer with a partner.

# **B** Plot

**7** Answer the questions.

- a  Where did the murder take place?
- b  Why did Winston leave the city?
- c  What did Daniel think about Tricia's project for the geography class?
- d  What did Daniel tell Tricia on the way to his house?
- e  What is the offshoot of Carban investigating?
- f  Why doesn't Daniel want his mother to know about this investigation?
- g  Tricia is reading some documents about the Ivory Coast online. What language are they in?
- h  Why isn't Daniel interested in Tricia's friend Anthea?
- i  Where was Tricia's father when she searched his computer?
- j  Tricia read a report by a specialist. What was the specialist worried about?
- k  What does Tricia's father do when he finds out about Daniel?
- l  What did Daniel do after he left school?

**8** With a partner define the following in your own words.

- a  carbon trade
- b  a carbon sink
- c  organic food
- d  the Kyoto Protocol
- e  greenhouse gas emissions
- f  a tailings dam

**9** Read the text about mining and the dangers and choose the correct word for each space.

Daniel is a member of Carban (a)............. is an organization that campaigns against the carbon trade. The carbon trade enables rich countries and companies to go on polluting the environment without paying any (b)............ . If they had to pay, they (c)............ more careful about pollution. Governments do nothing because they don't want to upset the global corporations – the people with the real (d)............ .

At the moment, Carban is investigating a big carbon-trade deal in (e)............ . They think it is being financed by a (f)............ company. The deal is worth millions of pounds. The company says it is building a dam to produce electricity but Carban doesn't believe this. A lot of people from a mining company, Afcob, are working for them. Also the (g)............ for the dam is an old mine. Daniel finds out the name of the company. It is called Tricolas. Tricia is (h)............ because Tricolas is her father's company.

| | | | |
|---|---|---|---|
| a | ① what | ② which | ③ who |
| b | ① punishments | ② attention | ③ penalties |
| c | ① would be | ② would been | ③ were being |
| d | ① pollution | ② energy | ③ power |
| e | ① Africa | ② America | ③ England |
| f | ① British | ② American | ③ African |
| g | ① lake | ② site | ③ earth |
| h | ① happy | ② excited | ③ upset |

**10** Daniel says you can find out about the carbon trade on the carbon trade watch website. With a partner find out some facts about the carbon trade on the Internet. Then tell the class.

## C Language

**11** Match the following expressions with their meanings.

[a] The thought crossed my mind.  
[b] She'd go crazy.  
[c] That rings alarm bells.  
[d] It's a scam.  
[e] They can trace stuff back to me.  
[f] What are you on about?

[1] What are you talking about?  
[2] It's a dishonest way of getting money.  
[3] They can connect things to me.  
[4] I thought about that.  
[5] She would be very angry.  
[6] That worries me.

**12** Complete the questions with the passive form of the verbs and then answer the questions.

[a] What / cobalt / use for?

_____?

_____

[b] When / the Kyoto Protocol / sign?

_____?

_____

[c] How many / countries / it / sign by?

_____?

_____

[d] What / some eucalyptus trees / burn for?

_____?

_____

[e] Who / Afcob / own by?

_____?

_____

## Practice Reported Speech

**13** Read the sentences in the bubbles and report what the characters said.

> Drive into the canal or I shoot.

> We won't talk. Please don't kill her.

> Do you know that Daniel's mother is dead?

> What are you talking about?

## Practice the Past Perfect

**14** Compete the sentences with a phrase from below and the past perfect.

- write an email to Carban
- go out to get some bread and things for lunch
- give a talk in the geography class
- learn he was behind the scam

(a) Daniel invited Tricia to his house after she _____.

(b) Before he died, Winston _____.

(c) Before the explosion, Daniel _____.

(d) Tricia searched her father's computer after she _____.

## Practice the Conditional

**15** Complete the sentences.

(a) "If your father didn't work so hard, the family _____," Tricia's mum said.

(b) If a company processed the stuff in a tailings dam, it _____.

(c) If the minerals from the tailings dam got into the Sassandra River, _____.

(d) If Tricia told the police about her father's company, he _____.

(e) If Tricia lied to Daniel, she _____.

**1** Tricia has designed a leaflet to hand out at the supermarket. Complete the leaflet with the words below.

were    airplane    organic    pesticides    packet    plastic

# How far has your food traveled?

This ..................... of beans at your local super-market comes from Kenya and has traveled 4,333 miles to get here. The beans ..................... picked five days ago. They have been packed in ..................... and have traveled by truck and by ..................... .

These ..................... carrots have traveled six miles from a farm near you. They were picked yesterday. They have never been sprayed with any ..................... .

Think before you buy!
Visit the Farmers' Market this Sunday
At Midsummer Common

**2** Where does the food you eat come from? Do some research and find out. Create your own leaflet.

**3** You read about carbon sinks in the story. Carbon sink projects are a threat to rainforests. Why are the rainforests important? Do the rainforest quiz and find out. Check your answers on the Internet.

EVERY SECOND A FOOTBALL FIELD OF RAINFOREST DISAPPEARS

ⓐ Because of tropical deforestation \_\_\_\_\_ of species are dying every day.

   ① 20%   ② 40%   ③ 50%

ⓑ It is estimated that it will take tropical forests \_\_\_\_\_ years to disappear.

   ① 30 to 50   ② 100   ③ 1000

ⓒ At least \_\_\_\_\_ of modern drugs come from the rainforest. Most were discovered and used by indigenous peoples.

   ① 5%   ② 10%   ③ 25%

ⓓ In one year, fires from the Amazon alone produced \_\_\_\_\_ tons of carbon dioxide.

   ① 500 million   ② 5 million   ③ 50 million

ⓔ There are \_\_\_\_\_ edible plants found in nature and we use only 150 of them.

   ① 20,000   ② 10,000   ③ 75,000

**4** In the story, environmental issues are important to Tricia and Daniel. Write a short paragraph about an environmental issue that interests you and illustrate it.

**請問你是在什麼時候知道自己想要走上寫作這條路的？**

其實我倒想說我記不起來什麼時候想要封筆過。我最早的作品是一齣戲劇，那是我和家人在聖誕節表演的戲碼，我當時是八歲。即使在從事其他事情時，我始終知道自己是作家。除了能夠坐下來寫東西，其他的事情都像是在打發時間。

**你提到戲劇，那你目前還有在寫劇本嗎？抑或只是寫小說？**

我寫了很多英語讀本的故事，也會寫劇本，因為我喜歡這種挑戰，能夠透過劇中人物的語言行為來呈現人物的性格。這和寫小說很不一樣，而當你目睹到演員們正在飾演你所創造出來的角色時，是非常令人興奮的。

**你會如何開始一部小說的寫作？**

我不會坐等靈感上門。我常常會找一個議題來下手，例如會讓我感到憤怒或憂慮的事情。接著，我會開始設計角色，誰會與這個議題關係密切？什麼樣的人又會受到影響或是被牽連進去？

**為什麼你會寫這篇小說？**

現在有很多資料都討論到了環保和碳交易的問題，而且我多年來一直對這個議題很有興趣。

**你去過非洲嗎？**

我去過北非幾次，有一次還搭船一路繞行非洲抵達肯亞，所以對非洲大陸有很深的感情。我覺得非洲所發生的事，對我們所有人來說都是關係密切的。

# I

**P. 11**

　　五月十二日星期四，在這世界上兩個遙不可及的角落裡，有兩件看似風馬牛不相及的事在同一時刻裡發生。

　　「好巧喔⋯⋯」翠希雅說道。她回顧著那一個時刻，然後閉上了嘴巴。

　　「什麼事情好巧？」媽媽要她繼續說下去。

　　「巧得令人難以相信！」翠希雅繼續說道：「那兩件事是在同一天的同一時間裡同時發生的，你不覺得太巧了嗎？」

　　「我不覺得，我不去想這件事，我凡事只往前看，不想過去的事。」媽媽說。

　　「我一直在想，如果事情不是這樣的話，不知道會怎樣。如果當中有一件事沒有湊巧發生的話，不知道會怎樣？還有，如果我⋯⋯」翠希雅說：「媽咪，我知道人不應該活在假設性的問題當中，只是，我很好奇，如果不是那樣的話，事情又會變成怎樣呢？」

　　　*　　*　　*　　*　　*

　　其中的一件事情，是發生在一條塵土飛揚的紅土路上，這條路通往赤道非洲中心地帶的某個小村子。不過這整椿事件的目擊者，就只有加害人和兩隻非洲灰鸚鵡。當時響起了三次的槍聲，兩隻灰鸚鵡立刻驚叫起來，帶著朦朧的紅色尾部羽毛，從濃密的森林中飛騰起來，接著傳來一個重重而沉悶的聲音，那是一個男性屍體被拋到荊棘灌木叢上的聲音。

**P. 12**

　　在持槍行凶的歹徒的眼裡，這個死者並不是個人，而是一項工作或任務。這些傢伙根本不把他當人看，而差遣他們前來行凶的幕後使者也是這麼認為。不過看來他們錯了。

　　每一個人都有名有姓，而且都有屬於自己的故事。這個橫死的人名叫溫斯頓，在一家跨國大公司裡服務，最近才剛遭到解雇。他心裡很驚惶，所以才離開了大都會，來到這條塵土飛揚的紅土路上，想逃到紅土路盡頭的村落裡。

　　他是在這個村落裡出生的，後來前往首都求學，在拿到學位後，便一直留在那裡工作。他在城裡娶了妻子，並育有兩名子女。妻兒都很擔心他，因為做妻子的知道有些非法的勾當正在進行，但是為了孩子著想，她的口風始終很緊，什麼都沒說。

　　溫斯頓的妻子是一位賢妻良母，當那名男子來到她家時，她就知道出事了。那名男子很寡言，沒有多說什麼，只知道他叫「清道夫」。他是星期四上午兩名持槍凶手當中的一位，兩人在非洲行凶後便爬回停在紅土塵沙路上的越野車。

「清道夫」並沒有敲溫宅的大門，而是直接破門而入。他沒有表明身分，但來意已經很明顯。他想要溫斯頓一家人閉上嘴巴。最後，他達到了目的，利用「恐懼」讓對方的閉嘴。

P.13

「清道夫」專門利用人類的恐懼心理來達到目的，他的工作是替人清除禍患。溫斯頓就是個禍患，所以被他清除掉。他現在闖進溫宅，想向溫太太傳達的訊息很清楚：他掌握了她和孩子們的行蹤。

溫夫人對這些都了然於胸，為了保住孩子們的性命，她只好守口如瓶，而她也清楚自己無法挽救丈夫的性命。看來一切都為時已遲。在溫斯頓的死訊傳來之前，她便悽然落淚了。溫斯頓還來不及離開城市，他的腳都還沒踏上紅土沙路，便已成為槍下亡魂。

溫夫人雖然深愛著老公，卻要隱忍不說，不但現在不能說，而且永遠也不能吐露。她得為孩子們著想，而「清道夫」就是仗著這一點才敢如此為所欲為。不只是他，買通他的那一票公司高層，也都吃定了這一點。

### 沉默不語

- 溫夫人決定閉嘴以免惹到「清道夫」，你可以想到哪一次你也選擇閉嘴嗎？或是在什麼時候最好是什麼都別說？

P.14

那家公司知道，人們一定會注意到溫斯頓消失了，也一定會前來查問。溫斯頓的人緣很好，朋友很多。而「清道夫」犯了一個錯誤，他以為沒有人會發現屍體，他想屍體會先受蟲蟻的侵蝕，然後雨水會來沖刷。只要溫夫人不說出去，一切都會神不知鬼不覺，他以為自己已經順利達成任務。然而，他一點也不了解溫夫人。

溫夫人很機警，她深愛著孩子，也很在乎丈夫。她雖然沒有提到「清道夫」這個名字，卻默默地採取了行動。就在男子到她公寓「拜訪」後的第二天，她一如往常地上市集，不過這一次她悄悄地和一個魚販講了話。這名魚販的小姨子剛好嫁給了溫斯頓的一位同鄉，於是消息悄悄地傳回了村子裡。當天，村民們便傾村而出，沿著紅土塵沙路一路搜尋，最後找到了屍體。

公司給出了一套說詞，他們表示溫斯頓患有憂鬱症，後來又發表聲明說，溫

斯頓因為讓公司的帳目兜不攏，所以被炒了魷魚。他們暗示溫斯頓吃裡扒外，儘管沒有人可以真正告訴他。公司還說溫斯頓已經消失了。

**P.16**

公司以為那個地方交通不方便，屍體不會很快就被發現，但人算不如天算，村民們說當時羊群正在荊棘叢附近吃草，就被一隻小羊發現了屍體。好死不好，就被羊群找到了屍體。

公司沒有料到，溫夫人會請人放出羊群沿路前進。她和孩子們還很安全，因為公司以為這只是因為運氣欠佳，「清道夫」也這樣認為，他認為溫夫人一定嚇得不敢吭聲，更沒想到她敢做出反擊。是羊群找到屍體的，只能怪運氣不佳。

於是公司又給了另一套說法，新的解釋是溫斯頓是自殺身亡的。這一番說詞令人不解，因為一個要自殺的人怎麼會在路上飲彈之後，還縱身跳入荊棘叢裡，更何況身旁根本就沒有槍枝。村民們暗地裡說著這些疑點，因為他們也有孩子。他們很清楚兩名持槍男子決非善類，他們知道「清道夫」那一幫人會怎樣對付他們。然而紙包不住火，人們談論著疑點，事情就這樣傳開了。

**P.17**

現在回到五月十二號星期四，「清道夫」正在紅土塵沙路上的森林裡。他上了越野車，撥了電話。他在和公司辦公室裡的人通話，對方只是簡單地說了聲「很好」，然後就掛了電話。公司這邊的人放下話筒後，立刻打了另一通電話到英國，電話那頭的男子在聽到後說道：「很好！就當這件事沒發生過，要確定沒有人會發現事情的真相，懂吧？」

「我知道！」遠在非洲辦公室裡的這名男子答道，他現在置身在象牙海岸這個小國的一個叫阿比姜的城市裡。

「如果事跡敗露，公司就完蛋了。」位在英國的男子叮嚀道。

「沒有人會知道真相的，」在阿比姜的男子一邊說，一邊望向潟湖延伸而去的高樓大廈，看著遠處的高原，「這一點我很確定！」

**p.18**

「那就好！」置身英國的男子又說：「我想今年年底會有一筆獎金。」他說罷便掛電話。顯然他不喜歡多講廢話，想講的話講完就可以結束談話。他這個人就是這樣不說多餘的話。而就在他說話之際，另外有一些人正在採取行動。

### 祕密

- 你有祕密嗎？
- 有人曾經跟你透露過祕密嗎？
- 什麼時候守住祕密是好事？而什麼時候守住祕密卻可能不是好事？

至於在五月十二日星期四這天所發生的第二件事又是什麼呢？事情發生在英國劍橋市的一所學校裡，時間是午飯前的最後一堂課，翠希雅・強生正在地理課上發表她的研究計畫：

**P.20**

「首先，我要提出以下這些事實：

1. 英國食物運送的距離，要比十五年前多了 50%。
2. 在過去十五年來前，食物的運送在道路運輸成長中佔了 33%。
3. 目前在英國，道路運輸是溫室氣體（二氧化碳）排放仍在持續增加的唯一原因。

「我想我們可以印製一份傳單，告訴大家食物運送到超市會花上多少哩程數。」她繼續侃侃而談：「我們可以把真相公布出來，讓人們知道食物的運送要飛上多少英哩的路程。」

「這是不是表示，高麗菜是自由飛行到西班牙的？」班上最愛寶寶的彼得問道。

他的那幫死黨咯咯作笑，但沒有人回答他的問題。

「現在我們拿兩種蔬菜來做個比較。第一種是在這條路上的超市買到的這一包豆子，它們來自肯亞，運送了 4,333 英哩才來到我們這裡的。豆子在運送的五天前採收，然後噴上化學藥品，以防在運送途中變色，最後用塑膠包裝起來，透過空運和陸運到這裡。」翠希雅說。

「看來它們應該在西班牙放個假，好好休息一下。」彼得說。

**P.21**

「第二種蔬菜是星期天在本地仲夏公地的生鮮農市裡買來的有機胡蘿蔔，外面只包了個紙袋子，是在上市的前一天才採收的，從產地運送到這裡只有六英哩的路程。它們只在田裡沖洗過，不會噴灑任何的化學藥劑。」

翠希雅在發表結束後坐了下來。她知

道自己這次的表現還不錯，她是費了好大的功夫才蒐集到這些資料的。地理老師亞許里小姐很滿意，班上的迴響也很熱烈，一致同意籌錢印製傳單，然後拿到超市外面發送。

接下來又發生了一件事。在下課鈴響後，翠希雅把書收進書包，打算去吃午飯時，丹尼爾·馬希穿過教室，朝翠希雅·強生走過來，和她講起話來。

丹尼爾·馬希是全校公認最酷的男孩，他的頭髮很黑，有一雙綠色的眸子，彈起吉他來簡直就像是吉他之神吉米附身一樣。這個丹尼爾·馬希是很多女孩子心目中的白馬王子，但他卻從來不跟班上的女生說話。

**P.22**

這真是前所未有的一刻，翠希雅·強生在班上並不算是頂漂亮的女生，她不但就像她自認為的那樣不夠漂亮，而且頭髮很普通，身材也不夠理想。然而，十八歲且大她六個月的丹尼爾·馬希卻走過來和她談論她的研究計畫。

「翠希雅，這很酷，我們應該要給超市施加些壓力，這很重要。」他說道。

翠希雅笑笑地點了點頭，可是卻又一句話都說不上來。

「我還有一些事情想跟你談。」他說。

「是嗎？」翠希雅說。

「等一下有沒有空到我家？」

翠希雅點了點頭。除非她被綁起來，或是躺在醫院裡，不然怎麼會沒空去丹尼爾‧馬希的家呢！班上還沒有人受邀去過丹尼爾的家，而且從小時候就一直這樣了。丹尼爾‧馬希竟邀翠希雅去他家，這可是一件破天荒的事！這是五月十二日的第二個事件——故事就由這個事件展開。

# II

**P.23**

「你對碳交易的了解有多少？」丹尼爾問道，一邊往後壓，躺在椅子上，蹺起兩隻椅腳。要是換成翠希雅或哥哥尼克在家裡做出這種坐姿，就會被媽媽唸，但馬希太太卻好像不太在意這種事。的確，丹尼爾的媽媽在許多方面都和她媽媽很不一樣，她是職業婦女，但翠希雅的媽媽沒有工作，只有偶而會到幾個委員會裡晃晃，和人們交際，喝一堆咖啡，如此而已。

**父母**

- 你的父母會對你所做的事抱怨嗎？
- 他們希望你是怎麼做的？

馬希太太一直忙於工作，因為丹尼爾的父親在他兩歲時就過世了，他們需要經濟來源。翠希雅對丹尼爾的爸爸一無所知，在前往丹尼爾家的一路上，丹尼爾跟她提到了自己的父親。

「所以你等一下就不要問到我爸爸的事喔。」他說。

**P.24**

「這是很傷心的事！」她一邊說，一邊想到學校裡都沒有人知道丹尼爾的事。大家雖然都很喜歡丹尼爾，可是他從來不說自己的事。

「是啊，我媽還是很想念他，不過我對我爸沒有印象，所以沒有任何回憶可想。對了，她是建築師。」

「誰？」翠希雅有點分神地問道。

「我媽。」丹尼爾說。

「噢，好厲害！」她答道，心想難怪以前都沒有見過丹尼爾的媽媽。他媽媽沒有時間和其他媽媽那樣一起做些事情。

她心想他們住的房子應該是很新，但其實不然。他們住在典型的維多利亞式街巷裡，她的很多朋友也都住在像這樣的街道裡。不過翠希雅一直都知道，她自己的家和同學的家不一樣。她的家雖然很寬敞，而且又是新的，但卻是採用紅磚式的傳統建築風格。她家有很多圓柱，車庫設計得很像鴿舍，出入口很大，大門是用鍛鐵打造的，門上面有爸爸的名字字首。

她覺得丹尼爾的媽媽才不會設計出這樣的房子，她想丹尼爾一定會嘲笑她家的那些裝飾文字，還有石頭門柱上的獅子和獨角獸。

**P.26**

丹尼爾家的外觀看起來和街上其他住家沒有兩樣，但屋子裡面的牆都打掉

了，創造出一個寬敞的開放式生活空間。裡面的牆壁都漆成紅色，灑滿了從房子兩端的窗戶所射進來的光線，其中一面牆排了一列列的書，書架上斜倚著兩個吉他盒。

在廚房的一端有一張松木製成的大桌子，現在她和丹尼爾就坐在那裡，桌上有一堆零亂的書報雜誌，地板上還掉了幾本書。在書堆中擺著一台電腦。丹尼爾進門後，便忙不迭地查看電子郵件。

丹尼爾的媽媽正在用白酒、番茄和大蒜料理食物，似乎不太在意兒子把東西弄得一團亂，不像翠希雅的媽媽那樣，一看到廚房的桌面上都是女兒的資料時，就會大呼小叫。

她媽媽泰瑞莎・強生喜歡每樣東西看起來都井然有序，這表示她們家常常要重新裝潢，不停地添購新的椅墊和窗簾，讓房子看起來好像是沒人住過一樣。朋友每次來她家鎮時，都會說她家好乾淨，她已經能聽出來言外之意：這樣不是很自然。

P. 27

但她媽媽就是喜歡這樣，所以她也不能怎樣。她覺得丹尼爾的家比較像個家，比起自己的媽媽，他媽媽似乎比較懂得放鬆。

### 放鬆

- 你覺得你是個容易放輕鬆的人嗎？
- 哪些事裡會讓你心情放鬆？又有哪些事情會讓你焦躁？

在翠希雅第一次去丹尼爾家討論可以採取什麼行動來防止全球暖化後，過了兩天，轉眼來到星期六的上午。她的父母要和一些客戶去賽馬場。為了這個場合，她媽媽還特地到倫敦添購了一套新的行頭，因為她爸爸的公司是活動的贊助商，她媽媽說自己得打扮得像樣。也因此翠希雅這一天可以自由地待在丹尼爾家，強生太太很高興女兒交了新朋友，不用一個人待在家裡。

翠希雅也很高興，她不敢相信自己和丹尼爾竟然這麼快就熟絡起來。在學校，當他們走在走廊上時，丹尼爾甚至還會把手臂搭在她的肩膀上。

P. 28

連班上最漂亮的金髮美女蒂芬妮，都會停下腳步望著他們走過。蒂芬妮不知道丹尼爾正在討論有什麼方法可以讓人們盡量購買在地的食物，但翠希雅在乎的並不是這個，她已經陷入情網了，而且最後發現有人看出了她的心思。生命中沒有一刻會比此時此刻更美好的了。她努力把心思拉回來，想聽清楚丹尼爾在說什麼。

丹尼爾把坐姿往前挪了挪，敲起鍵盤，說道：「你知道『碳交易』嗎？」

翠希雅思索了一下，她一無所知。

「那麼，你對京都了解多少？」丹尼爾又問。

「京都是日本的一個地方，曾經是首都，有很多古老的廟宇和神社。」翠希雅說。

「很有趣。」丹尼爾說。

**P.29**

翠希雅笑了笑，說道：「各國領袖曾經在京都這個地方開過會，還簽署了一份協議書，用來防止氣候變化，減少溫室氣體，而美國沒有簽署。」

「你講得差不多了。一九九七年，共有一百八十個國家簽署了《京都議定書》，呼籲三十八個工業國家減少溫室氣體的排放。」丹尼爾說。

「哇，你真是個專家！」翠希雅笑逐顏開起來，「溫室氣體的元凶是二氧化碳。」

「沒錯！」丹尼爾同意道。

「但我還是不清楚碳交易是什麼。」翠希雅繼續說道。

「噢！」丹尼爾把身子往前傾，不再讓椅腳蹺起來。翠希雅幾乎可以感覺到他的呼吸輕輕拂過她的臉頰，而他的皮膚散發出蜂蜜般的味道。她很想觸摸他的臉，她渴望他會吻她。她努力把心思拉回來。

「《京都議定書》的目的是要全面減少溫室氣體，但是有些國家顯然無法達到

目標。他們沒有因為傷害地球而受到懲罰，而是提出一套計畫，也就是所謂的碳交易。基本上來說，這是指那些沒有污染的國家和企業，可以把他們的『低碳積點』賣給污染國家的公司，用這種方式來控制世界各地的溫室氣體。」丹尼爾說。

**P.30**

「但這並不表示富裕的國家可以買到把碳繼續排放到空氣中的權力吧？」

「沒錯，事實的確如此。當初的構想是，如果要排放污染氣體，就要付費，這樣就可以減少排放量，然而人們會鑽漏洞，這個構想並未發揮真正的作用。而這也是我們的組織『碳絆』何以會發起活動，呼籲禁止碳交易的原因。我們希望迫使那些企業降低排放量。」

丹尼爾在空閒時會擔任「碳絆」的志工，而翠希雅對該組所知甚少。

**閒暇時間**

- 你閒暇時間會做什麼？
- 你擔任過志工嗎？你喜歡做什麼樣的志工？

「你可以在這個專門監督碳交易的網站上找到很多資料，」丹尼爾告訴她說：「有很多環保人士對正在進行的事憂心忡忡，像是投資尤加利植林地，以便燒木生產木炭。他們的觀點認為，種植樹木能夠產生『碳匯』，可以吸收碳──然而，燒木取炭的作法，只會在空氣中排放出更多的碳。」

（譯註：carbon sink，是指從大氣中

清除二氧化碳的過程或機制，和「碳源」（carbon source）的概念相反。「匯」是指物質歸結之所，海洋、土壤和森林是地球上主要的碳匯處。）

**P.32**

「這聽起來很糟糕。」

「這種事一直在發生，如果依然故我，在我們有生之年，整個的亞馬遜雨林就可能變成沙漠。」

「那會不會……」翠希雅開口問道。

「會不會讓全球暖化的速度加倍？會！會不會讓地球變得無法住人？當然會！」

「各國政府為什麼不想辦法？」

「統治世界的不是政府，而是那些跨國大企業。」丹尼爾回答：「他們享有既得利益，所以默不作聲。不過事要是愈來愈嚴重，他們可能就不會坐視不管了。不過也許我比其他一些我認識的活動分子要樂觀一些。」

「這種情況令人很憂心。」翠希雅說。

「這也是我們為什麼要站出來付諸行動的原因。」丹尼爾說道，他不停敲著鍵盤，身子略向前傾，皺起了眉頭。

「怎麼了？」翠希雅問。

丹尼爾讀著一封電子郵件，一邊搖著頭。他做了些記錄後，把郵件刪除掉。

「到底怎麼啦？」翠希又問了一次。

「我等一下在跟你說。」丹尼爾指了一下他媽媽，小聲說道。

大約一個小時後，馬希太太走進書房工作。翠希雅說：「你現在可以說了吧，是怎麼一回事？」

**P.33**

「我不想讓媽媽知道，我怕她會擔心。『碳絆』的一個分會開始調查非洲一個新的碳交易合約，這次的交易很大筆，我們很確定這是一筆非法交易。我們推測幕後的金主是英國的一家公司，只是我們還沒有找出是哪家公司。」丹尼爾說。

「為什麼這會讓你媽媽擔心？」翠希雅問道。

「有幾個原因，比方說，我們取得那些資料的方法可能不是很合法……」

「你們是非法入侵電腦？」翠希雅問。

丹尼爾點點頭。「雖然我們在非洲安排了一位人手來追查，但他生病了或什麼的，只好回來。或是像他說的，他也可能被警告了。」

「事情很嚴重嗎？」

「這是當然的，他們可能會因此損失幾百萬英鎊。」丹尼爾說：「這些人會使出一切手段，以防事跡敗露。正因為這樣，我才不能保留任何記錄，那很不安全。我不可能讓媽媽知道這件事，她要是覺得我正在做的事情很危險，她會瘋掉的。」

## 危險

- 你曾經覺得身陷險境過嗎？
- 如果你覺得朋友正在做很危險的事，你會怎麼做？

**P.34**

翠希雅環顧了舒適的廚房，她想不出來還有什麼地方會比這裡安全。

「這個聽起來是不是有點太戲劇性了呢？」她問道。

「或許吧，」丹尼爾笑了起來，「不管怎樣，我會確定不會被追蹤到我這裡。」

「那封電子郵件寫了什麼？」翠希雅問道。

「裡面提到有一位名叫溫斯頓的告密者，他從我們的網站上找到我們，於是跟我們聯絡上。他說他應該讓我們知道他公司所幹的那些勾當，我們想他是要跟我們揭發一些事情。他是礦物學家，這讓我們不禁質疑：為什麼一家宣稱要建水壩的公司，會需要用到礦物學家？」

「那是一家建水壩的公司？」翠希雅問。

「那是他們的說詞，但那裡地處象牙海岸的中心位置，要拿到那個地方的資料不是很容易。」丹尼爾告訴她說：「如果他們真的要建一座水力發電用的水壩，提供電力給象牙海岸最大的城市阿比尚的話，那就沒問題。水力發電是一種乾

淨的能源，所以才會有花數百萬美元蓋一座碳匯的計畫。可是，這個計畫有一些疑點，很多人覺得根本不是要蓋碳匯。」

**P.35**

「有什麼樣的疑點？」翠希雅問。

「首先就是，這家公司找了很多曾經替愛富可企業工作的人。愛富可是一家惡劣的礦業公司，他們曾經在剛果雇用童工開礦，又在查德污染了大片的雨林區。而且愛富可只是一家掛名的公司，由十幾家小公司所共有，他們的企業總部都設在一些像是巴哈馬和開曼群島這樣的地方，那些地方以境外帳戶聞名。」

「那就無法追蹤到源頭了。」翠希雅看了很多驚悚小說，知道境外帳戶的事。

「所以我們要查的是，為什麼他們會選擇位於象牙海岸中心地帶的這小段河流，我們想知道他們是不是真的在蓋水力發電用的水壩。麻煩的是，那地方前不著村，後不著店，而且所有的道路都有警衛看守，所以很難查出他們到底在裡頭做什麼。」

「那麼那個礦物學家呢？」

「溫斯頓？對！這件事很卑鄙。他準備跟我們說實情，他說他很憂心。後來在幾天前，公司把他炒魷魚，如今已經死亡，公司說他是自殺的。」

「好可怕啊！」

「那不可能是自殺。村民在草叢裡找到了他的屍體，他是被槍殺的，他們忘了把槍留在現場。」

翠希雅的眼睛有點酸痛，時間已經過了兩個小時，她正打算找象牙海岸的礦

產資料。她在網路上看到的資料大都是法文，雖然她在學校的法文考試拿到了A，但她沒有學過礦業術語，所以閱讀那些資料有點困難。

象牙海岸擁有各種資源——像是鑽石、黃金、石油和天然氣等。然而，這個國家卻出奇的貧窮，大部分的人民以種植為生。他們種的東西是地理課上會看到的那些農產品，例如可可、咖啡、香蕉、玉蜀黍和鳳梨。

她問丹尼爾：「你知道象牙海岸一度擁有西非最大的森林嗎？但現在卻不太看得到什麼森林了。」

P.37

「都被砍伐殆盡了嗎？」他問。

「我想是的。那個法文字的正確意思是什麼我不太確定，但上面所說的意思就是這樣。現在，除了一座國家公園裡的一小塊林地之外，全部的林地都變成了……這個字的英文要怎麼說？……我想就是『半沙漠』。這真是太可怕了！」她補充道。

「那礦業呢？」丹尼爾問道。

「我找到資料了，不是很好找。大部分的礦產都是由一家國營企業所掌控。很多地方都對象牙海岸的鑽石採取禁運措施，因為他們把賣鑽石的錢拿來用在打仗上。那裡有戰爭嗎？」

丹尼爾聳了聳肩，「我想不是戰爭，也許是有一些反抗軍和政府交戰。媽媽可能知道，不過她不會想知道為什麼我這麼好奇。還有其他的嗎？」

P.38

翠希雅閃過一個念頭：或許是因為她正在修法文，所以丹尼爾才會找她來幫忙。她暫時不去想這個問題，儘管這個想法繼續糾纏著她。至少她正在和他「共度良辰」！反之，那位真正的大美女、假日時還會去當模特兒的安瑟亞，就沒有這樣的「殊榮」。安瑟亞一直「肖想」著丹尼爾，但丹尼爾從未邀她回家喝咖啡過。

就在前一天，翠希雅假裝不經意地提到安瑟亞這個名字。

「真受不了像她那樣的女生，沒什麼大腦！」丹尼爾說：「我在走廊上遇到她們時，她們聊的東西真是無趣。」

翠希雅當時有一種背叛朋友的感覺，但她還是笑了出來。安瑟亞算是她的朋友，儘管她覺得她們的友情好像都是單方面的。她會幫安瑟亞寫功課、修改家庭作業，而在學校的餐廳用餐時，安瑟亞會允許翠希雅加入她們一桌。

## 友誼

- 你會在朋友身上尋找什麼樣的特質？
- 忠誠很重要嗎？回想一下你忠實對待朋友或朋友忠實對待你的經驗。

**P.39**

翠希雅輕輕嘆了一口氣，不再自問丹尼爾到底喜不喜歡她，而是把心思拉回網頁上。她看到一些和鈷有關的資料。

「那裡有在開採鈷嗎？」她問道。

丹尼爾差點要跳過桌子，「就是這個東西沒錯！鈷價值連城，製造長效電池、放射線等等之類的東西，都要用到鈷。每個人都想要得到鈷。」

「在六〇年代時，一個叫蘇倍雷的地方有產鈷礦，後來因故停止了開採，但他們並未説明原因。」

「我得打電話給一個人。」丹尼爾説。

「打給誰？」翠希雅問。

「約翰。」丹尼爾解釋道：「他是我的一位朋友，我們去年在一場抗議集會上認識的。他在東英格蘭大學教書，是這方面的專家，也是碳絆的會員。沒有人比約翰更最懂礦物的了。」

一直到丹尼爾談話結束，翠希雅都聽不太懂內容，她大都只能説「是！」、「對！」和「真的嗎？」來做回應。

丹尼爾接下去又説：「不是有個網站嗎？它的內容一定會讓你很吃驚。它的密碼是什麼？等等，我剛剛有抄下來。」

翠希雅有看到他當時用筆寫下一組文字和數字。

**P.40**

「他怎麼説？」丹尼爾放下電話後，翠希雅問道。

「他給了我一個網站，好幫助我揪出藏鏡人。擁有人是一家銀行，約翰認為他們可能牽涉到碳交易計畫的資金籌措。」

丹尼爾鍵入密碼，開始讀著螢幕上的文章。

「那個地方是叫什麼來著？」他問道。

「蘇倍雷，位在沙山卓河。」翠希雅回答。

「這裡有張地圖，上面指出了計畫要蓋在蘇倍雷的水力發電水壩。這是個大工程，我把它印出來。」丹尼爾説。

他把印出來的地圖交給翠希雅。翠希雅皺了皺眉頭。

「這很奇怪，我剛剛才看過另一個要在蘇倍雷蓋水力發電水壩的國際大工程資料，但是和上面所指出的地點不一樣。這……」

她看了看另一張地圖，「礦坑是位在這裡。」

「兩座水壩？這不合理。」丹尼爾説。

翠希雅繼續回到她的筆記上。

「我們來看，幾年前有個要在蘇倍雷蓋水壩的計畫，但因為會對當地居民和附近的國家公園造成破壞，所以作罷。後來雖然有一家法國公司又再度勘查了這項計畫，但地點不在這裡，而是在蘇倍雷的北邊。」

丹尼爾查看了一下地圖。

**P.41**

「至於那家銀行所要籌資興建的水壩，是位在蘇倍雷的南邊。」翠希雅繼續説道。

「那座礦坑就在這個地方。」丹尼爾説。

「他們為什麼要選在礦坑的位置上蓋水壩？」

「我不知道，我要問問約翰。」丹尼爾説。

丹尼爾又撥了電話給約翰。這一次他在電話上沒說什麼，只是頻頻點頭。

「怎麼樣？」翠希雅問。

「約翰認為這是一座礦尾壩。」丹尼爾說道。

「那是什麼？什麼是礦尾？」翠希雅問。

「礦尾是指銅、銀等任何礦物從地下被挖走之後所留下來的所有東西。在以前，人們採礦的方式造成嚴重的破壞，只取走看到的東西，然後就把其他的東西都堆在礦坑四周，或是倒進河裡。他們習慣在河中築水壩，弄出一個深水潭，然後把不要的東西都倒進去，這就是尾礦壩。」

「那現在為什麼要蓋新的水壩？」翠希雅問。

「尾礦壩裡面往往堆了很多在今天可謂價值連城的東西。」

「就像鈷嗎？」翠希雅說。

「完全正確。」丹尼爾同意地說道：「而且從水中把鈷取出來，要比從地底下把它挖出來省錢多了。」

P.42

「這樣的作法有什麼不對嗎？」翠希雅問。

丹尼爾告訴她說：「那家公司雖然可以因為碳匯而從政府手中拿到錢，但這並不是減碳的方法。這是錯誤的作法，更何況在尾礦壩裡處理鈷，會隱藏很大的危機。約翰說，這可能會引發各種的災難，像是在蓋亞那的一個案例中，他們把氰化物倒進了河裡。因此，這個作法很不好。」

「但這個作法卻可以讓企業削爆……」翠希雅說。

「進帳個幾百萬美元是跑不掉的。」丹尼爾邊說邊回到電腦螢幕上，然後繼續閱讀。

「就是這個沒錯！」他喊道，「我想我已經找到幕後的那家公司了。」

翠希雅立刻往他的肩膀靠過去。

「是什麼公司？」她問道。

「崔克拉斯。」丹尼爾說。他把頭轉向翠希雅後，問道：「嘿，你還好吧？你怎麼臉色發白？」

「我只是吃壞肚子。」翠希雅一邊奔向廁所，一邊含糊地說道。

# III

P.43

翠希雅記不得上一次進爸爸的書房是什麼時候的事了。倒不是書房禁止別人進入，而是家裡一直有一條常規：爸爸在工作時，不准進他的書房。

「不要讓你爸爸分心。」媽媽會說：「如果他不這樣努力工作，我們就不會擁有這美好的一切了。」

因為書房的門永遠都是關著的，而且裡面也沒什麼有趣的東西，所以翠希雅沒進去過。不過這一次，她打開書房的門，走了進去。書房和家裡的其他房間迥然不同，沒什麼裝潢，不是很舒適。裡頭沒有什麼東西，只有一張黑檀木桌子，上面放了台電腦。翠希雅心想，黑檀樹是生長在雨林裡的古木，卻被人類砍下來製作成這樣一大件家具，丹尼爾要是看到了，不知道會說什麼。

書房裡還有一個金屬製成的灰色檔案櫃，醜不拉幾的。翠希雅還記得，有一次媽媽建議不妨換個木製的檔案櫃，這樣看起來一定漂亮多了，結果惹來爸爸的譏笑。

「不過是個存放文件的地方，誰會管它好不好看？」他說。

P.44

媽媽於是嘆了口氣，並做了讓步。對她的設計團隊來說，這間書房的確是禁止進入的。

整個書房裡最讓人感到舒服的東西，就是那張黑色的大皮椅了，椅子下面還有一個很搭調的腳凳。除此之外，書房裡唯一的裝飾物就是一個很大的玻璃紙鎮，那是爸爸不知道在什麼比賽中獲勝的獎品，重量著實不輕，翠希雅到現在都還拿不太動。

翠希雅的父母去了賽馬場，一整天都不在家，而哥哥尼克也在劍橋大學裡，所以翠希雅知道，現在進書房是非常安全的。不過即使是這樣，她發現自己還是躡手躡腳走進書房，彷彿她不想讓房子聽到她偷溜進去的聲音。

她坐在爸爸的書桌前，打開電腦。

崔克拉斯，在丹尼爾說出這個字時，她就知道那是爸爸的公司了。這個名字，是爸爸拿她和哥哥的名字所組合而成的：Tricia 和 Nicholas。當然，爸爸不是所有這一切的幕後主使者，不是嗎？當然不是啦！

電腦有密碼，當然，是有密碼的。翠希雅試了各種密碼。是數字嗎？是爸媽的生日？還是尼克或是她的生日？結果都不是，這太容易破解了。爸爸最在意的還有什麼？

**密碼**

- 你的電腦有設密碼嗎？
- 你選擇的是什麼樣的密碼？

P.46

翠希雅往後一坐，環顧房間四周。牆上有一張照片，是爸爸和一票政客在下議院前的合照；另外還有一張照片，是他在紐馬克賽馬場的贏家圍場裡拍的，是他和合夥人以及他名下的那匹馬的合照。

翠希雅還記得，比賽一結束，爸爸立刻把那匹馬賣了。據爸爸說，那個買賣賺進了一大筆錢，讓他樂翻了。翠希雅覺得，那匹馬在父親的眼裡不過是一個買賣的物品，就像那個昂貴的紅酒一樣，他買來後根本沒有要喝，又像他從拍賣會上標得的那些畫，一旦到手就鎖進銀行裡。爸爸唯一的興趣，似乎就是成為贏家，賺進更多的錢。

翠希雅的目光不斷在房間裡徘徊，

直到她看到了爸爸的另一張照片。這次是他在遊艇上的照片，她心想，他真正喜歡的另一樣東西，就是開著他的遊艇「隼鷹號」到處飆船了。「隼鷹」？突然間她笑了起來，可不是嗎，隼鷹是全世界速度最快的動物，可以邊飛行邊獵食。

翠希雅敲了「peregrine」這個字。賓果！她進入了爸爸的電腦裡了。

當她瀏覽過那些檔案後，原來那一點喜悅的感覺頃刻間煙消雲散。崔克拉斯、蘇倍雷，電腦裡隨處可見這些字眼。她可以打開這些檔案，找到丹尼爾所需要的所有資料，但接下來嗎？難道她真的要背叛父親，把資料交給丹尼爾？但如果她不大義滅親的話，又會發生什麼事？水壩要是建成了，會有多少人死於非命？

**P.47**

翠希雅知道，不管如何，她都要把事情搞清楚。於是，她開始詳讀起來。

所有的東西都在這裡面，包括採礦報告，還有如何處理尾礦壩的水的細節。其中有一份報告這樣寫道，「一潭骯髒的紅水，價值數百萬」。他們不但不是要建造碳匯來蒐集碳，好讓地球得以喘息，反而是要蓋毒水的人工湖，犧牲成千上萬人的性命，來換得幾個人的暴利。

看來他們的計畫是蓋一座新水壩，然後利用水力來處理礦坑的毒水，過濾後再把水放回河裡。裡面有一份由當地的專家所寫的檔案，翠希雅猜想那個專家會不會就是溫斯頓。檔案裡說這名專家十分憂心，他認為水中含有的危險化學物質，例如氰化物和砷等，隱含著極大

的危險性。他向公司報告說，尾礦壩的工程會把那些化學物質釋放到沙山卓河裡，危害人們的性命。

這篇報告的日期呢？就在四天之前，翠希雅繼續讀下去，想看看是否有人對這一點做出的回應。過了一個小時，她終於找到了線索。在另一個叫做「任務」的資料夾中，公司下了一道命令給一個名叫「清道夫」的人，要他去處理一件「小小的內部事務」，而這個「事務」的名稱就叫溫斯頓。

**P.48**

「我知道你們可以用一樣的方式來達成這項任務，」她的爸爸這樣寫道：「你們都知道，這個資料絕對不能外流出去，不然會對公司危害甚大。這些資料的來源一定要永遠封鎖起來。」

這時，傳來了一個聲音，翠希雅跳了起來。屋子裡有其他人，不是只有她一個人。

翠希雅把所有檔案複製到隨身碟裡，然後關上所有的資料夾。她不知道爸爸會不會發現有人開過他電腦裡的檔案。但是，他怎麼會這樣想呢？這是他在家裡的電腦，沒有人會去動他的電腦。

翠希雅於是關了電腦，躡手躡腳地走出書房，來到走廊。

「哈囉。」她一邊叫道，一邊鎮定下來。

「翠希雅，」哥哥喊道：「是你嗎，老妹？因為保全沒有啟動，所以我想家裡面一定有人在，可是家裡好安靜，我以為你在睡覺。」

「我只是在看書。」她說。

翠希雅走進廚房裡，哥哥正在廚房替

自己泡咖啡。

「你怎麼會在家裡？我還以為你在學校裡考試呢。」她說。

**P.49**

「我今天放假，去打橄欖球比賽，結果慘兮兮。」尼克解釋道：「我看把球塗上膠水，他們也抓不住一球。欸……」他忽然住嘴，「你怎麼了，老妹？」

翠希雅知道自己眼眶泛紅，快哭出來了。

「是誰欺負你啦？他對你做了什麼事？你要我去揍他嗎？」尼克問。

翠希雅破涕為笑。雖然他們兄妹的感情不是特別親，但她很喜歡哥哥。兄妹兩個人的個性很不一樣，自從哥哥去寄宿學校念書，而她堅持進入當地的高中之後，他們兩個人就好像住在不同的星球上一樣。尼克上了寄宿學校後個性就變了，變得讓翠希雅不喜歡，也就是因為這樣，翠希雅才不願意去讀寄宿學校。

她不想變得像尼克那樣，周遭的朋友都是有錢的公子哥兒，成天談的不外乎是冬天要到哪兒滑雪，或是夏天要去

什麼地方乘船等等的。翠希雅不喜歡滑雪，坐遊艇也會暈船，她喜歡的度假方式是和三五個好友躺在海灘上，然後玩玩水。她和尼克沒有什麼共通點，但他終究是她哥哥。

「尼克，我可以相信你嗎？」翠希雅終於開口說話。

「你這是什麼話呀，我是你老哥耶。」

「我知道，我只是不知道該怎麼辦才好。你想，你要是發現爸爸捲進了很不好的事情，你會怎麼做？」

「這是哪個問卷調查裡頭的笨問題呀？」

「我是說真的，而且是很不好的事，是違法的事情。」

「你這是什意思？」哥哥一邊把牛奶倒進咖啡裡，一邊說道：「爸爸不會去做那種事的。」

「那萬一他要是做了呢？」

「翠希雅，你把事情說清楚！」

翠希雅於是把事情說了出來。碳交易的事、蓋水霸的計畫、尾礦壩，還有溫斯頓的事，她都一五一十地說了出來。不過，她沒有說她把所有的資料都複製到了她口袋裡的隨身碟。

「這無法證明爸爸指使人去殺掉那個傢伙的，光是那些文字並不能當作證據，那在法庭上站不住腳。」尼克說。

「這裡是廚房，我們正坐在桌子旁，不是法庭！」翠希雅說。

**P.51**

「正是這樣，所以事情絕對不能說出去！」尼克說道：「你在爸爸電腦上所看到的所有資料，都得留在這個屋子裡，你明白嗎？」末了他又加上一句：「要是

101

被人發現了，爸爸就完蛋了。」

## 家人

- 如果你發現家人涉及了非法事件，你會怎麼做？
- 你覺得家人應該互相掩護嗎？還是你覺得應該據實以告？

「我知道，所以我才很難過。」

「也是，發現這種事情，並不是好事。你的那個朋友叫什麼名字？」尼克自己的臉色也都有些蒼白了。

「丹尼爾。」翠希雅說。

「丹尼爾。他是你男朋友嗎？」

「大概是吧，他的全名是丹尼爾‧馬希。他人很好。」翠希雅覺得自己臉紅了。

「那你要確保這個叫丹尼爾‧馬希的傢伙不會發現崔克拉斯就是爸爸的公司。你想，他會不會懷疑到什麼？」

P.52

「不會吧，我什麼都沒說。」翠希雅回答。

「那就好，現在你要答應我，決不會把這件事告訴丹尼爾！」尼克說。

「好。」翠希雅緩緩說道。雖然她覺得這麼做不太對，但她怎麼可以背叛自己的父親呢？

「還有，尼克，你也要答應我，不要跟爸爸提這件事，不要讓他知道我知道實情。」她補充道。

「我當然不會說，不可以讓他知道我們兩個都知道這件事。」尼克說。

翠希雅這下子才放鬆了下來。

「去做一些讓自己放鬆的事，不要再想這些事了。去看電影或什麼的，找你

的女性朋友出來，做做女孩子們會做的事。」尼克說。

「女孩子們會做的事？」翠希雅說：「像是聊化粧品或鞋子之類的話題嗎？這我沒興趣。」

「那你想做什麼就去做什麼，能把這些事情忘掉就好。那是爸爸的世界，那些事情我們實際上也沒有權利知道。」尼克說。

翠希雅坐在床上，一邊讀著法文課要上的卡繆的《異鄉人》，一邊心想：尼克的看法或許是對的。她應該跟丹尼爾講話，但那樣她就得撒謊了，這種事很困難。她討厭說謊，而且她也不會說謊，一定會被丹尼爾識破的。那她就不要跟丹尼爾見面，但她去學校就一定會碰到他。她怎麼想都行不通，而最難過的事，是不能見到丹尼爾。

# IV

P.53

馬丁‧強生的心情真是盪到了谷底，他輸了錢，不只是因為輸錢令他心煩，他更討厭的是那種輸的感覺。他痛恨輸的感覺。更嘔的是，他押的馬跑得像頭暈船的驢，而老婆所押的馬卻頻頻獲勝。

只見一場比賽又接著一場比賽，泰瑞莎覺得很有趣。她都是看馬的名字來下注的，有的名字會讓她回想起某個假期，或是想起某隻認識的小狗。反之，馬丁‧強生卻是對這些馬很熟。

他看著老婆，老婆笑得很開心，正舉起滿手的鈔票向他揮舞。他得承認，泰瑞莎看起來仍然風韻猶存，雖然她的開銷很大，總是不停地在添購行頭、旅

行或是去做美容三溫暖。他想不通，怎麼會有人需要一個訂價二千塊英鎊的手提包？但不可諱言的，他的客戶很喜歡她，她雖然已經是兩個孩子的媽了，但看起來跟當初嫁給他的樣子沒有兩樣。

這時，他的行動電話響了。

「喂。」他沒好氣地說。

「爸，我是尼克。」

「有什麼事？我現在和朋友在一起。」

「我們講話會有人聽到嗎？」尼克問。

**P.54**

馬丁走到贊助商貴賓室的窗子邊，這個貴賓室的家具花了他一些銀兩。

「現在不會有人聽到了，什麼事？」他說。

「是翠希雅，她和一個朋友發現了崔克拉斯公司的一些事。」尼克說。

「你這話是什麼意思？」馬丁問。儘管天氣很溫暖，而且他西裝畢挺，卻仍感到一身冷顫。

「非洲的水壩，所有的事情，還有被槍殺的人。」兒子這樣告訴他。

「怎麼會呢？」他又問道。

「她看到了你的檔案。」

**P.55**

「你說她怎樣？」馬丁發覺到自己正在大吼大叫，他看到泰瑞莎的目光朝他的方向移來，於是連忙壓低嗓門。「為什麼會這樣？她在幹什麼啊？」他問尼克。

「她在和學校裡一個叫丹尼爾·馬希的男孩研究環保問題，那個男孩打算把非洲的那些事情挖出來，結果就找到了崔克拉斯這個名字。翠希雅知道是你的公司，所以就看了你的檔案。」

「這個笨女孩！她要那些資料幹嘛？」

「她也沒有要幹嘛，只是可以想像她心裡很不舒服。不過她已經答應過我，不會告訴她男朋友，她現在待在家裡頭。」尼克說。

**.56**

「還好你也在家裡。可是，你怎麼會在家？你怎麼沒有去學校？」

「我是剛好回家，我剛去參加比賽。」

「那就好。」馬丁想到他的檔案要是被放到網路上的話，一切就完蛋了。

「爸爸，這些事一定要讓你知道。」

「當然，尼克，你真是好孩子，你這樣做就對了。」

「不過不要讓翠希雅知道，我答應過她，不要把這件事告訴你，所以你就裝做什麼都不知道吧。」

「我了解。」做父親的說道。

「不是你下命令去做掉非洲那個傢伙的，對吧？」尼克問，語氣聽起來突然變得像小孩子。

「我當然不會這樣做啊，我只是給他封口費，但他是個奇怪的傢伙，我猜他是欠了黑道的錢。你知道在非洲這種事的下場會很慘，他們到處在火拼，他的死和我沒有任何關係，你可絕對不能認為是我下的手。」

「當然不會，爸爸。」

「那就好。我和你媽媽什麼時候去看你呀？」父親問道，口氣聽起來愉快多了，「你學期要結束了，也該好好慶祝一番，可以週末去巴黎度個假，住麗池酒店，順便交交朋友。」

馬丁隨便向客戶編了個理由，然後去到一處安靜的走廊，打幾通電話，以免

103

隔牆有耳。很快地，他手上就多了一個地址，接著他又撥了另一個電話。

「『清道夫』在城裡嗎？」他問：「很好，我還有任務要給他。」

「要弄一個小小的瓦斯外洩事故？」馬丁望向窗外的賽馬場，但他眼裡看不到任何的馬匹。他眼前所看到的，只有樹林中間那一潭黑水，水裡頭所含的礦物，足夠讓一個國家飛黃騰達。水會變黑，是因為水裡頭含有礦物，才讓原本的紅水變成黑色的。這潭水就是他的夢想、他的未來。

「小小的瓦斯外洩事故？這個點子太妙了，算是間接傷害吧？」他想了一下，又說：「有人死掉，總不是好事，但又有哪個地方不會死人呢？去告訴『清道夫』，最重要的就是弄到那台電腦，而且不會被發現，他知道該怎麼做。還有，愈快愈好，告訴『清道夫』，如果我明天就能拿到那台電腦，賞金加倍。」

接著他又聆聽了片刻，然後說：「沒錯，很好。」

他俯視前方一匹匹奔馳的賽馬，滿場的群眾在歡呼，而他的思緒卻飄蕩到千里之外。不過賽馬還是要繼續賭下去，他得回到客戶那裡說說笑笑。他做了個深呼吸，臉上戴上笑容。

「這次是誰贏了？」他問：「是高飛？幹得好，老兄。我想再來杯香檳。」

他向匆忙而過的女侍彈了一下手指，但沒瞧她一眼。他現在就像是在舞台上睡著了的演員一樣，雖然知道正確的台詞和動作，但他的魂已經不在。他的心思一直在女兒翠希雅的身上，他想，到底要拿她怎麼辦才好？

## V

P.58

到了星期天上午，翠希雅整個人變得很安靜，但媽媽並沒有察覺出來，因為媽媽頭痛欲裂，那是因為香檳在作怪，於是決定整個上午都待在床上。翠希雅的爸爸在書房裡，房門緊閉著，尼克也返回學校去了。

早餐過後，翠希雅坐在臥室裡望著電腦，她想打電話或是寫電子郵件給丹尼爾，因為丹尼爾已經傳了幾通簡訊給她，看起來有點擔心她。這很不公平，她明明這麼想見丹尼爾，卻又不知道見面時該說什麼才好。

她捶了捶枕頭。「丹尼爾，這種事怎麼偏偏發生在我們身上？怎麼每件事都變得這麼棘手？」看來這樣也不是辦法，她得見見他。

翠希雅走在米爾路上，這時傳來了爆炸聲，她立刻朝丹尼爾所住的莫森路飛奔而去。警察正在隔開人群，但翠希雅鑽過了封鎖線。就在她轉過街角進入莫森路時，有人冷不防地攔腰一把抓住她，把她拉到了籬笆後面。是丹尼爾，他的臉哭得都紅了。

「丹尼爾……」翠希雅先開腔了。

「他們把媽媽害死了，她在屋子裡。」

「什麼？」

P.60

「我出門去買中午要吃的麵包和食物，只有媽媽留在家裡，後來當我要回去時，突然就爆炸了，整間屋子耶。現在這件事情已經上了新聞，他們說是瓦斯外洩所造成的。」

「我不懂。」翠希雅說道。

「他們是怎麼知道的？」丹尼爾問。

「我不知道。」翠希雅說。是爸爸做的嗎？她有些懷疑，但尼克答應她不會說出去的。可是爸爸，他不會這樣做，會嗎？他可以把丹尼爾的家炸掉嗎？可以殺了他媽媽嗎？

「他們可能竊聽到約翰的電話了。」丹尼爾說。

「我們得馬上離開這裡，要讓他們認為你也死了，你要躲起來。」翠希雅說。

「怎麼躲？躲去哪裡？」丹尼爾問。

「我不知道。」翠希雅說。

「我們需要一輛車，公車站和火車站都有監視器。」丹尼爾說。

「尼克的車子在家裡，學期還沒結束，他用不到車。我們可以開他的車，你會開車嗎？」翠希雅說。

「我會，我上個月拿到駕照了。但是，我們要躲去哪裡？」丹尼爾問。

「給我一些時間想想。你就待在這道籬笆後面。」翠希雅說。

她瞧了瞧屋子，那邊沒有人。「這地方暫時還很安全，我現在就去把尼克的車子開過來接你。」

## P.61

家裡面很安靜，翠希雅很快就在走廊的抽屜裡找到了尼克的鑰匙。不過正當她要進入自己的房間時，爸爸打開書房的門走了出來。

「翠希雅，是你嗎？最近還好嗎？」他開始說話了。

翠希雅沒有回答，只是把他推回書房裡。她不知道爸爸怎麼會知道丹尼爾的，但她突然覺得爸爸要為整件事負責。

「是你做的嗎？你知道丹尼爾的媽媽已經死了嗎？」她問。

「你在講什麼呀？」爸爸說道。就在這時，翠希雅看到了丹尼爾的那台電腦就放在父親的桌子上。

「不！不！」她大叫了起來，「你怎麼可以這樣？」

「翠希雅，別叫！」父親喝斥道。

翠希雅立刻奪門而出，然後跳進尼克的車子裡。爸爸隨後追出去，但她毫不理會地發動了車子。雖然她還沒有駕照，但尼克在放假時教過她開車，所以她知道如何開車。

她小心翼翼地開著車，速度很慢，最後來到了丹尼爾等待的地方。丹尼爾於是鑽進駕駛座，把車子開向外環道。

「我們要去哪裡？我們為什麼要這麼做？我不知道自己在做什麼！」他說。

「我們去找個安全的地方，待上一兩天，想出個辦法看要怎麼做。」翠希雅說：「有些事我要告訴你，我知道崔克拉斯公司的老闆是誰，也知道是誰殺了溫斯頓和炸掉你家的。是我爸爸！」

## P.62

### 下一步要怎麼做

- 你有過下一步不知道如何做的經驗嗎？
- 你當時是怎麼解決的？和夥伴分享一下。

那個叫做「清道夫」的人正沿著鄉間馬路緩緩地開車，尾隨著那輛銀色小轎

105

車。「這輛車子實在太好跟了。」他心想。前方車子的駕駛似乎沒注意到後面跟了一輛車子，看來這件事很好解決。

P.63

「清道夫」是個不喜歡把事情搞砸的傢伙，那場爆炸幹得很漂亮，但後來卻發現那名男孩沒有在屋子裡。他當時待在同一條街上的另一棟房子裡，從窗戶邊監視整個情況。那名男孩才是發現資料的人。看來他還得再製造一起意外事故，弄得就像是那名男孩因為喪母、悲傷過度，所以才自殺。他不知道車上的那名女孩是誰，但她不是問題，弄死一個人和弄死兩個人，是一樣簡單的任務。

他就這樣緩緩開著車，一邊看著地圖，一邊計畫著。

馬丁・強生很擔憂，「你想他會完成任務嗎？」他問。

電話那頭的男人認為這是想當然耳的事情。

P.64

「不，這不是我想要的結果，你沒辦法聯絡上他嗎？」馬丁說。

「沒辦法。『清道夫』只有在完成任務後，才會跟我們聯絡。這樣做對誰都好。」男子對他這樣說道。

「你一定要讓他住手，」馬丁吼了起來，「他要追殺的那個男孩正開著我兒子的車，而我女兒就坐在車子裡頭。我竟然派殺手去追殺自己的女兒！」

馬丁這時閉上嘴，因為他聽到書房外面傳來了聲音。他走出書房查看，是妻子泰瑞莎，她一定是在走廊上聽到他的

談話，然後昏厥了過去。他連忙掛上電話，把妻子扶到客廳。

「你都聽到了？」妻子恢復意識後，他問道。

「我從來就不想知道你怎麼那麼會賺錢，花不完的錢，我從來不過問。」她用冰冷的眼神看著丈夫，「我相信你，就因為我相信你，所以不曾過問。」

「這個問題我會處理的，我會讓他住手，翠希雅一定不會有事的。」馬丁說。

「你是說丹尼爾・馬希綁架了你的女兒？」刑警慢條斯理地說，對自己的遣詞用字非常謹慎。

馬丁・強生和總警司很熟，捐過大筆錢給警方的慈善活動，算是個有權有勢的人。

P.65

「我想他很可能就是莫森路爆炸案的肇事者，我女兒說他對製造炸彈的設備很有興趣，我相信他是某個組織的成員。我女兒曾說再也不想看到他，但這小子卻偷走我兒子的車，而且綁架了我的女兒。她才十七歲，我實在很擔心她，她現在的處境一定很危險。」馬丁說。

翠希雅被綁架的新聞立刻上了媒體，每個人都開始尋找那輛銀色的車子，有很多男女也都被攔住問話。

尼克從朋友那裡得知了這個消息。

「那不就是你妹嗎？」朋友問。

尼克打電話回家給媽媽。他們靜靜地談著，之後尼克到了最近的警察局做了一份冗長的筆錄。

「這很有趣，也證實了馬希太太所說的事。」督察說。

「她不是在爆炸案中死了嗎？」尼克問。

「她運氣很好，她那時人正在花園裡，只是昏了過去，應該沒事。」督察說。

「那我妹妹呢？」尼克問。

「這件是就很棘手，我們派出所有的警力去尋找你妹妹的下落，但能否及時找到她還是個問題。」督察說。

# VI

P.66

丹尼爾和翠希雅從車上收音機裡的新聞報導中聽到了這則報導：

「警方目前正全力緝捕一名可疑的恐怖分子，警方相信他就是今天上午發生在劍橋市那件爆炸案的幕後策劃者。他的姓名迄今仍未公布，但警方認為他可能綁架了劍橋市的少女翠希雅·強生。如果有人看到一輛銀色車子，應立即和警方聯絡，車子的車牌號碼是……」

翠希雅關掉收音機，「怎麼變成綁架案了？」

「是你爸爸這樣對警方說的。」丹尼爾說。

「那我們要怎麼辦？」翠希雅問。

丹尼爾把車停了下來，前方的道路又平又直，旁邊有一條很深的運河和道路平行著，而四周都是濕黏黑土的田地，種著一排排的翠綠植物，看不到任何房子，是一個很荒涼的地方。

「如果他們認為我是恐怖分子，那一定會不管三七二十一先對我先開槍再說。」丹尼爾緩緩說道。

「如果我在就不會。他們不會對我開槍，而且我隨身碟裡頭有證據，我們『一定會』沒事的。」翠希雅說。

「我已經不知道我是不是還在乎什麼了，我一直想到我媽。」丹尼爾說。

這時，一輛黑色小轎車突然開過來，停在他們旁邊，接著一個男的從車子裡走出來。只見他高頭大馬，一頭灰髮，戴了一付黑色墨鏡，把半張臉都遮蓋住，而且身上還帶了槍。

這名「清道夫」一邊拿槍對著丹尼爾，一邊進了他們車子的後座。

P.68

「這真是個好地方，你們省了我不少力氣。」清道夫說完又把槍指著翠希雅。

「把車子開進運河裡，不然我就開槍。」他對丹尼爾說。

「我們不會說出去的，請不要殺她。」丹尼爾說。

「我也不想開槍，把事情弄成像意外事件比較簡單。如果沒有必要，我也不會開槍。」清道夫說。

「就像你射殺溫斯頓一樣。」翠希雅說。

「你們這些笨孩子，哪來的這麼多問題！現在開車。」清道夫說。

丹尼爾把車子打到一檔，然後慢慢駛離路面，直接開向運河。

翠希雅一輩子還沒碰過這麼可怕的事。水很快就要把車子吞沒，清道夫在車子完全駛出路面時就跳出了車子。水潮壓過來，讓她和丹尼爾無法打開車門。

「你可以打破車窗嗎？」丹尼爾問。

翠希雅奮力用鞋子敲擊車窗。

「太硬了，打不破。」她說。

# VII

P.70

尼克坐在往家裡駛去的警車上，這時警察正用行動電話在通話中。

「一個農民在鳥類保護區附近看到一輛你們所說的銀色汽車，我們已經派遣警用直昇機過去。」

「是翠希雅嗎？」尼克說：「都是我的錯，我還那麼相信爸爸。」

「你不用為你父親的事負責，這件事你做得很對。」警察說。

「可是還來得及嗎？噢，翠希雅！」尼克說。

# VIII

P.71

水不斷地漲上來，車子裡就快要沒有空氣了。

「我很抱歉。」翠希雅說。

「沒關係，你並不知情。」丹尼爾說。

「我愛你。」翠希雅說。她心想，她就快死了，終於可以說這句話了。

丹尼爾握住她的手。「別說話，我們要盡量節省空氣。」他說。

翠希雅把他的頭往上托，「我很會潛水。」她說。

接著，一切在瞬間沒入黑暗之中，所以她並沒看到有陰影從頭頂上晃過，也沒有聽到直升機著陸時所發出的聲音。

# IX

P.72

當總警司回到警局裡時，馬丁·強生正坐在裡面作筆錄。

「我們已經找到令嬡了。」警司說道。

「她還……」馬丁一時之間為之語塞。

「還活著是嗎？是的，她還活著。」警司說：「幸虧我們及時趕到，要是再晚一步的話，你女兒和她朋友恐怕就性命難保。」

馬丁·強生用雙手抱住頭，哭了起來。

「我們也逮捕了一個叫『清道夫』的人，我想你應該認識這人。看來至少有七個國家的警方想要和他談談，我們以引發爆炸和謀殺未遂的罪名逮捕他，但除此之外，他在其他很多案子裡也被控告謀殺，我想『你』或許可以在一些案件上協助我們。」警司補充道。

# X

P.73

翠希雅在醫院裡可說是訪客不斷，尼克和媽媽每天都來報到，丹尼爾和他媽媽也差不多每天都來。

丹尼爾如今成了舉國皆知的英雄人物，照片也出現在每家報紙上。

他媽媽說：「我們家整天電話都沒停過，電視台的人想採訪他，」這時她笑了起來，「他討厭這種陣仗！還有信件，有好幾袋，真是太瘋狂了。」

翠希雅想跟著一起笑，丹尼爾的人是很好，可是事情沒有這麼單純。因為想殺害他和他媽媽的人，是『她』爸爸。

就是因為『她』把事情告訴尼克，他們才差一點沒命的。

這些細節沒有上報，但對她爸爸的報導就很多。她爸爸現在已經被收押，警方在她醫院門口安置了警力，以保護她免受媒體的干擾。還有，由於她爸爸把電腦裡的記錄都銷毀，所以被她複製到隨身碟裡的那些資料就變得很關鍵。

「人們都認為你也是英雄。」馬希太太繼續說道：「你做出了一個很困難的抉擇。」

「但這是我的錯，把事情告訴了尼克。」翠希雅說。

**P.74**

「他是你哥哥，你信任他，而他最後也去跟警察報案了，是他救了你。」馬希太太說。

「是這樣沒錯。」翠希雅說。

她還記得困在車裡的那個時刻，當她覺得就快要溺死的時候，心裡卻是快樂的，因為丹尼爾愛她，她也愛丹尼爾。而現在，事情就沒那麼單純了。

「你已經活了過來，我和丹尼爾也是，還有，你很快就會把壞人送進牢裡。只要想這些就行了。」馬希太太說。

「謝謝你。」翠希雅說。看來馬希太太很了解她。

「你和丹尼爾不久就要上大學了，事情一定會有所轉變的。」馬希太太說。

**轉變**

- 想想看，你的人生曾經在什麼時候有過轉變？當時發生了什麼事情？
- 你的人生在轉變的前後，有什麼不一樣？

許多事情都有了轉變，最讓翠希雅意想不到的，是媽媽的轉變。

「在遇到你爸爸之前，我是一個出色的祕書。」她說。

**P.76**

馬丁·強生失去了所有的財富，翠希雅和媽媽便搬到劍橋市另一頭的一間小公寓裡，泰瑞莎還找了一份工作，奇怪的是，她反而更快樂了。還有，尼克最後認為他和以前那些死黨毫無共通之處，於是開始認真讀書，找份工作。

丹尼爾離開學校後，就到一所媒體無法干擾的私立大學參加考試。他也找到了工作，還在一個電視節目裡發表氣候變遷的議題。他會寫電子郵件給翠希雅，但她從雜誌中可以知道更多他的事。雜誌上寫到，他即將和一位美麗的氣象學家一同遠赴北極。日子還要繼續過下去，她明天還要考試。

她打開書本準備唸書，這時手機嗶嗶作響，傳來了這樣一封簡訊：

祝你明天考試順利
愛你的丹尼爾

他並沒有忘記她。沒錯，人生是美好的。

# ANSWER KEY

## Before Reading

Page 7
**1** 1. b   2. a   3. c   4. b   5. a
6. c   7. b   8. a

Page 8
**3**
1. ☑ Thriller
2. ☑ A murder   ☑ A kidnap

**4** (Possible answers)
- **Daniel:** He has short dark hair. He's good-looking. He's wearing casual clothes. He seems to be in front of a computer. He looks friendly and he might like computers. Maybe he is a student or a computer programer.
- **Mr Johnson:** He is quite old. He's got short brown hair and a moustache. He is wearing a suit and he looks like a businessman. He is talking on the phone. He doesn't look very friendly.
- **Tricia:** She seems the same age as Daniel. She has shoulder-length blonde hair. She is pretty. She looks quite serious.

Page 9
**7**
a) leaflets
b) explosion
c) dam
d) global corporations
e) emissions
f) mine
g) memory stick
h) the races

## After Reading

Page 78
**1**
3, 2, 1
**2** ambitious, powerful, greedy, cold-hearted, secretive

**3** (Possible answers)

| Name | Martin Johnson |
| --- | --- |
| Nationality | British |
| Personality | He is ambitious and greedy. He will do nearly anything to get what he wants. |
| Business | He has his own company. He is involved in an illegal carbon-trade deal in Africa. |
| Likes | Money, power, success and his yacht. |
| Dislikes | Losing money |

Page 79
**4**
a) Winston
b) Martin Johnson
c) Tricia Johnson
d) Mrs Marsh
e) The Sweeper
f) Daniel Marsh

**5** (Possible answers)
- He's tall with gray air and dark glasses.
- He's called the Sweeper because he sweeps up problems.
- He's wanted by the police in seven countries.
- He shot Winston.
- He tried to blow up Daniel's house.
- He tried to drown him.

Page 80
**7** (Possible answers)
a) On a dusty red earth road that led to a small village in the Ivory Coast.

b) Winston left the city because he was afraid.

c) Daniel thought Tricia's project was cool.

d) He told her that his father was dead.

e) It's investigating a huge new carbon-trade deal in Africa.

f) He doesn't want her to worry about him.

g) French.

h) Because he thinks she hasn't got a thought in her head and is boring.

i) He was at the races with some clients.

j) The specialist thought there was a risk of dangerous chemicals getting in the water and if that happened people could die.

k) He calls the Sweeper.

l) He studied for his exams at a private college and got a job presenting a program on television about climate change.

**Page 81**

**9** a) 2    b) 3    c) 1    d) 3    e) 1
   f) 1    g) 2    h) 3

**Page 82**

**11** a) 4    b) 5    c) 6    d) 2    e) 3    f) 1

**12**

a) What is cobalt used for?
   It is used to make long-life batteries and radiation and stuff.

b) When was the Kyoto Protocol signed?
   It was signed in 1997.

c) How many countries was it signed by?
   It was signed by 180 countries.

d) What are eucalyptus trees burned for? They are burned to make charcoal.

e) Who is Afcob owned by?

It's owned by dozens of small companies with head offices in places that are famous for offshore accounts.

**13** (Possible answers)

a) The Sweeper told Daniel to drive into the canal or he would shoot him. Daniel said that they wouldn't talk and he begged the Sweeper not to shoot Tricia.

b) Tricia asked her father if he knew that Daniel's mother was dead. Tricia's father said that he didn't know what she was talking about.

**14**

a) had presented a project to her geography class.

b) had written an email to Carban.

c) had gone out to get some bread and things for lunch.

d) had learnt he was behind the scam.

**15** (Possible answers)

a) wouldn't have all these nice things.

b) would be dangerous.

c) people would die.

d) he would be sent to prison.

e) he would find out.

## Project Work

**Page 84**

**1** packet, were, plastic, airplane, organic, pesticides

**3**

a) 40%

b) 30-50

c) 25%

d) 500 million

e) 75,000

國家圖書館出版品預行編目資料

少年駭客之綠色事件簿 / Antoinette Moses 著
; 李璞良 譯. 一初版. 一 [ 臺北市 ]：寂天文化，
2012.8　面；公分 .

　中英對照
　ISBN 978-986-318-028-9 (25K 平裝附光碟片 )
　1. 英語　　2. 讀本

　805.18　　　　　　　　　101014424

■作者 _ Antoinette Moses　　■譯者 _ 李璞良　■校對 _ 陳慧莉
■封面設計 _ 蔡怡柔　■主編 _ 黃鈺云　■製程管理 _ 蔡智堯
■出版者 _ 寂天文化事業股份有限公司
■電話 _ +886-2-2365-9739　■傳真 _ +886-2-2365-9835
■網址 _ www.icosmos.com.tw　■讀者服務 _ onlineservice@icosmos.com.tw
■出版日期 _ 2012年8月 初版一刷（250101）
■郵撥帳號 _ 1998620-0 寂天文化事業股份有限公司
■訂購金額600 （含）元以上郵資免費　■訂購金額600元以下者，請外加郵資60元
■若有破損，請寄回更換　■版權所有，請勿翻印